"In Case You Haven't Noticed, I've Had A Hard Time Keeping My Eyes Off You Tonight."

"I'm sorry, but I'm having a difficult time believing you would be interested in me."

Hannah couldn't be more wrong. "Why wouldn't I be? You're smart and savvy and pretty damn brave to raise a child on your own and finish college at the same time."

"Keep going."

Logan could...all night. "You're a survivor and very beautiful, although you don't seem to know that. And that's not only hard to find in a beautiful woman, it's appealing."

"And?"

"Right now I'd like to kiss you," he blurted out before his brain caught up with his mouth. "But I'm not going to."

"Why not?" she asked, looking thoroughly disappointed.

"Because if I kissed you, I might not want to stop there."

* * *

From Single Mom to Secret Heiress is a Dynasties: The Lassiters novel—A Wyoming legacy of love, lies and redemption!

* * *

If you're on Twitter, tell us what you think of Harlequin Desire! #harlequindesire

Dear Reader,

I am happy to report that I was blessed with three children. Though they've all reached adulthood, I still retain fond memories of the pitfalls and pleasures of parenthood. My oldest daughter was an easy baby who slept through the night at six weeks, thanks to that attached pacifier known as the thumb, and she remained low maintenance throughout her formative years. My second daughter had a real pacifier and a penchant for losing it several times and wailing about it during the wee hours. She continued that course until the ripe old age of eighteen months, and she's definitely making up for it now due to the demands of her career. However, the serious sleep deprivation brought about by baby number two did not discourage me from having baby number three a little over two years later. And that baby happened to be my son, commonly referred to as "the male child." From the time he began to walk, he never stopped running or climbing or getting into trouble, and making mom's anger go away with an innocent smile.

Granted, all three presented challenges at one time or another during their childhoods, but I was lucky enough to have a fantastic husband who shared in the responsibility, and he did it without looking as shell-shocked as his wife. That's why I always marvel at stories of single moms—and dads—who struggle to balance budgets and child-rearing on their own, sometimes working two jobs to make ends meet. I'm sure most would love to wake up one morning and discover an unexpected fortune dropped into their laps.

And that is exactly what happens to widowed single mom Hannah Armstrong when she opens the door to a gorgeous attorney bringing tidings of a surprise inheritance—with a few conditions attached. Hannah certainly didn't bargain for becoming an overnight heiress, but more important, she didn't expect to be so darned attracted to another man, especially one as mysterious and sexy as Logan Whittaker. But when two people with emotional scars and serious chemistry join forces, anything can happen...even love.

I truly hope you enjoy this heartfelt story of hope and healing as much as I enjoyed telling it.

Happy reading!

Kristi

FROM SINGLE MOM TO SECRET HEIRESS

—

KRISTI GOLD

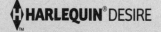

Special thanks and acknowledgment are given to Kristi Gold
for her contribution to the Dynasties: The Lassiters miniseries.

Recycling programs
for this product may
not exist in your area.

ISBN-13: 978-0-373-73313-2

FROM SINGLE MOM TO SECRET HEIRESS

Printed in U.S.A.

KRISTI GOLD

has a fondness for beaches, baseball and bridal reality shows. She firmly believes that love has remarkable healing powers and feels very fortunate to be able to weave stories of love and commitment. As a bestselling author, a National Readers' Choice Award winner and a Romance Writers of America three-time RITA® Award finalist, Kristi has learned that although accolades are wonderful, the most cherished rewards come from networking with readers. She can be reached through her website at www.kristigold.com, or through Facebook.

To my fellow Lassiter authors, particularly Kathie DeNosky, my good friend and brainstorming buddy. I can always count on you to have my back, as long as you've had your coffee. Couldn't have done this one without you.

One

What a way to begin the end of April—with limited funds and leaky plumbing.

Yet Hannah Armstrong couldn't quite believe her sudden change in fortune. Twenty minutes after placing the 5:00 p.m. service call, and hearing the dispatcher's declaration that they would *try* to send someone out today, her doorbell sounded.

She left the flooded galley kitchen and carefully crossed the damp dining-room floor that was littered with towels. After entering the living room, she navigated another obstacle course comprised of a toy plastic convertible painted shocking pink, as well as a string of miniature outfits that would be the envy of the fashion-doll world. "Cassie, sweetie, you have to pick up your toys before you can spend the night with Michaela," she called on her way to answer the summons.

She immediately received the usual "In a minute, Mama," which came from the hallway to her right.

Hannah started to scold her daughter for procrastinating, but she was too anxious to greet her knight in shining tool belt. Yet when she yanked the front door open, she was completely taken aback by the man standing on her porch. The guy had to be the prettiest plumber in Boulder. Correction. All of Colorado.

She quickly catalogued the details—a six-foot-plus prime specimen of a man with neatly trimmed, near-black hair that gleamed in the sun and eyes that reminded her of a mocha cappuccino. He wore a navy sports coat that covered an open-collared white shirt, dark-wash jeans and a pair of tan polished cowboy boots, indicating she'd probably pulled him away from a family function. Or quite possibly a date since he didn't appear to be wearing a wedding band.

"Ms. Armstrong?" he asked as soon as she stepped onto the porch, his voice hinting at a slight drawl.

Considering her ragtag appearance—damp holey jeans, no shoes, hair piled into a disheveled ponytail and a faded blue T-shirt imprinted with Bring it On!—Hannah considered denying her identity. But leaky pipes took precedence over pride. "That's me, and I'm so glad to see you."

"You were expecting me?" Both his tone and expression conveyed his confusion.

Surely he was kidding. "Of course, although I am really surprised you got here so quickly. And since I've obviously interrupted your Friday-night plans, please know I truly appreciate your expediency. Just one question before you get started. What exactly do you charge after normal business hours?"

He looked decidedly uncomfortable, either from the question or her incessant rambling. "Anywhere from two-fifty to four hundred regardless of the hour."

"Dollars?"

"Yes."

Ridiculous. "Isn't that a bit exorbitant for a plumber?"

His initial surprise melted into a smile, revealing dimples that would make the most cynical single gal swoon. "Probably so, but I'm not a plumber."

Hannah's face heated over her utterly stupid assumption. Had she been thinking straight, she would have realized he wasn't a working-class kind of guy. "Then what are you? *Who* are you?"

He pulled a business card from his jacket pocket and offered it to her. "Logan Whittaker, attorney at law."

A slight sense of dread momentarily robbed Hannah of a response, until she realized she had no reason to be afraid of a lawyer. She gained enough presence of mind to take the card and study the text. Unfortunately, her questions as to why he was there remained unanswered. She'd never heard of the Drake, Alcott and Whittaker law firm, and she didn't know anyone in Cheyenne, Wyoming.

She looked up to find him studying her as intently as she had his card. "What's this about?"

"I'm helping settle the late J. D. Lassiter's estate," he said, then paused as if that should mean something to her.

"I'm sorry, but I don't know anyone named Lassiter, so there must be some mistake."

He frowned. "You are Hannah Lovell Armstrong, right?"

"Yes."

"And your mother's name is Ruth Lovell?"

The conversation was growing stranger by the minute. "Was. She passed away two years ago. Why?"

"Because she was named as secondary beneficiary should anything happen to you before you claimed your inheritance."

Inheritance. Surely it couldn't be true. Not after all the years of wondering and hoping that someday...

Then reality began to sink in, as well as the memory of her mother's warning.

You don't need to know anything about your worthless daddy or his cutthroat family. He never cared about you one whit from the moment you were born. You're better off not knowing....

So shell-shocked by the possibility that this had something to do with the man who'd given her life, Hannah simply couldn't speak. She could only stare at the card still clutched in her hand.

"Are you okay, Ms. Armstrong?"

The attorney's question finally snapped her out of the stupor. "I'm a little bit confused at the moment." To say the least.

"I understand," he said. "First of all, it's not my place to question you about your relationship with J. D. Lassiter, but I am charged with explaining the terms of your inheritance and the process for claiming it. Anything you reveal to me will be kept completely confidential."

When she realized what he might be implying, Hannah decided to immediately set him straight. "Mr. Whittaker, I don't have, nor have I ever had, a relationship with anyone named Lassiter. And if you're insinuating I might be some mistress he kept hidden away, you couldn't be more wrong."

"Again, I'm not assuming anything, Ms. Armstrong. I'm only here to honor Mr. Lassiter's last wishes." He glanced over his shoulder at Nancy, the eyes and ears of the neighborhood, who'd stopped watering her hedgerow to gawk, before turning his attention back to Hannah. "Due to confidentiality issues, I would prefer to lay out the terms of the inheritance somewhere aside from your front porch."

Although he seemed legitimate, Hannah wasn't comfortable with inviting a stranger into her home, not only for her sake, but also for her daughter's. "Look, I need some time to digest this information." As well as the opportunity to investigate Logan Whittaker and determine whether he might be some slick con artist. "Could we possibly meet this evening to discuss this?" Provided she didn't discover anything suspicious about him.

"I can be back here around seven-thirty."

"I'd prefer to meet in a public venue. I have a daughter and I wouldn't want her to overhear our conversation."

"No problem," he said. "And in the meantime, feel free to do an internet search or call my office and ask for Becky. You'll have all my pertinent information and proof that I am who I say I am."

The man must be a mind reader. "Thank you for recognizing my concerns."

"It's reasonable that you'd want to protect not only yourself, but your child." He sounded as if he truly understood, especially the part about protecting Cassie.

She leaned a shoulder against the support column.

"I suppose you've probably seen a lot of unimaginable things involving children during your career."

He shifted his weight slightly. "Fortunately I'm in corporate law, so I only have to deal with business transactions, estates and people with too much money to burn."

"My favorite kind of people." The sarcasm in her tone was unmistakable.

"Not too fond of the rich and infamous?" he asked, sounding somewhat amused.

"You could say that. It's a long story." One that wouldn't interest him in the least.

"I'm staying at Crest Lodge, not far from here," he said. "They have a decent restaurant where we can have a private conversation. Do you know the place?"

"I've been there once." Six years ago with her husband on their anniversary, not long before he was torn from her life due to a freak industrial accident. "It's fairly expensive."

He grinned. "That's why they invented expense accounts."

"Unfortunately I don't have one."

"But I do and it's my treat."

And what a treat it would be, sitting across from a man who was extremely easy on the eyes. A man she knew nothing about. Of course, this venue would be strictly business. "All right, if you're sure."

"Positive," he said. "My cell number's listed on the card. If your plans change, let me know. Otherwise I'll meet you there at seven-thirty."

That gave Hannah a little over two hours to get showered and dressed, provided the real plumber didn't show up, which seemed highly unlikely. "Speaking of calls, why didn't you handle this by phone?"

His expression turned solemn once more. "First of all, I had some business to attend to in Denver, so I decided to stop here on the way back to Cheyenne. Secondly, as soon as you hear the details, you'll know why I thought it was better to lay out the terms in person. I'll see you this evening."

With that, he strode down the walkway, climbed into a sleek black Mercedes and drove away, leaving Hannah suspended in a state of uncertainty.

After taking a few more moments to ponder the situation, she tore back into the house and immediately retreated to the computer in her bedroom. She began her search of Logan Whittaker and came upon a wealth of information, including several photos and numerous accolades. He graduated from the University of Texas law school, set up practice twelve years ago in Dallas, then moved to Cheyenne six years ago. He was also listed as single, not that it mattered to Hannah. Much.

Then it suddenly dawned on her to check out J. D. Lassiter, which she did. She came upon an article heralding his business acumen and his immeasurable wealth. The mogul was worth billions. And once again, she was subjected to shock when she recognized the face in the picture accompanying his story—the face that belonged to the same man who had been to her house over twenty years ago.

That particular day, she'd returned home from school and come upon him and her mother standing on the porch, engaged in a heated argument. She'd been too young to understand the content of the volatile conversation, and when she'd asked her mom about him,

Ruth had only said he wasn't anyone she should worry about. But she had worried…and now she wondered….

Hannah experienced a surprising bout of excitement mixed with regret. Even if she had solid proof J. D. Lassiter was in fact her father, she would never have the opportunity to meet him. It was as if someone had given her a special gift, then immediately yanked it away from her. It didn't matter. The man had clearly possessed more money than most, and he hadn't spent a dime to support her. That begged the question—why would he leave her a portion of his estate now? Perhaps a guilty conscience. An attempt at atonement. But it was much too late for that.

She would meet Logan Whittaker for dinner, hear him out and then promptly tell him that she wouldn't take one penny of the Lassiter fortune.

At fifteen minutes until eight, Logan began to believe Hannah Armstrong's plans had changed. But from his position at the corner table, he glanced up from checking his watch to see her standing in the restaurant's doorway.

He had to admit, he'd found her pretty damned attractive when he'd met her, from the top of her auburn ponytail to the bottom of her bare feet. She'd possessed a fresh-faced beauty that she hadn't concealed with a mask of makeup, and she had the greenest eyes he'd ever seen in his thirty-eight years.

But now…

She did have on a little makeup, yet it only enhanced her features. Her hair hung straight to her shoulders and she wore a sleeveless, above-the-knee black dress that molded to her curves. Man-slaying curves that reminded Logan of a modern version of those starlets from days gone by, before too-thin became all the rage.

When they made eye contact, Hannah started forward, giving Logan a good glimpse of her long legs. He considered her to be above average in height for a woman, but right then she seemed pretty damn tall. Maybe it was just the high heels, although they couldn't be more than two inches. Maybe it was the air of confidence she gave off as she crossed the room. Or maybe he should keep his eyes off her finer attributes; otherwise he could land himself in big trouble if he ignored the boundary between business and pleasure. Not that he had any reason to believe she'd be willing to take that step.

Logan came to his feet and rounded the table to pull out the chair across from his as soon as Hannah arrived. "Thanks," she said after she claimed her seat.

Once he settled in, Logan handed her a menu. "I thought for a minute there you were going to stand me up."

"My apologies for my tardiness," she said. "My daughter, Cassie, had to change clothes three times before I took her to my friend's house for a sleepover."

He smiled over the sudden bittersweet memories. "How old is she?"

"Gina is thirty. Same as me."

Logan bit back a laugh. "I meant your daughter."

A slight blush spread across Hannah's cheeks, making her look even prettier. "Of course you did. I admit I'm a little nervous about this whole inheritance thing."

So was Logan, for entirely different reasons. Every time she flashed those green eyes at him, he felt his pulse accelerate. "No need to be nervous. But I wouldn't blame you if you're curious."

"Not so curious that I can't wait for the details until after dinner, since I'm starving." She opened the menu and began scanning it while Logan did the same. "I'd forgotten how many choices they offer."

He'd almost forgotten how it felt to be seated at a dinner table across from a gorgeous woman. The past few years had included a few casual flings for the sake of convenience with a couple of women who didn't care to be wined and dined. Sex for the sake of sex. And that had suited him fine. "Yeah. It's hard to make a decision. By the way, did you get your plumbing fixed?"

She continued to scan the menu. "Unfortunately, no. They called and said it would be tomorrow afternoon. Apparently pipes are breaking all over Boulder."

With the way she looked tonight, she could break hearts all over Boulder. "Do you have any recommendations on the menu?"

"Have you had bison?" she asked as she looked up from the menu.

"No. I'm more of a beef-and-potatoes kind of guy."

"Your Texas roots are showing."

She'd apparently taken his advice. "Did you check me out on the internet?"

"I did. Does that bother you?"

Only if she'd discovered the part of his past he'd concealed from everyone in Wyoming. *Almost everyone.* "Hey, I don't blame you. In this day and time, it's advisable to determine if someone is legitimate before you agree to meet with them."

"I'm glad you understand, and you have quite the résumé."

He shrugged. "Just the usual credentials."

"They certainly impressed me."

She undeniably impressed him. "Have you eaten bison before?"

"Yes, I have, and I highly recommend it. Much leaner and healthier than beef."

"I think I'll just stick with what I know."

Her smile almost knocked his boots off. "Perhaps you should expand your horizons."

Perhaps he should quit sending covert looks at her cleavage. "Maybe I will at some point in time." Just not tonight.

A lanky college-aged waiter sauntered over to the table and aimed his smile on Hannah. "Hi. My name's Chuck. Can I get you folks something to drink? Maybe a cocktail before dinner?"

Bourbon, straight up, immediately came to Logan's mind before he realized booze and a beautiful woman wouldn't be a good mix in this case. "I'll have coffee. Black."

Hannah leveled her pretty smile on Chuck. "I'd like a glass of water."

The waiter responded with an adolescent grin. "Have you folks decided on your meal?"

She took another glance at the menu before closing it. "I'll take the petite bison filet, medium, with a side of sautéed mushrooms and the asparagus."

Logan cleared his throat to gain the jerk's attention. "Give me the New York strip, medium rare with a baked potato, everything on it."

Chuckie Boy jotted down the order but couldn't seem to stop staring at Hannah as he gathered the menus. "How about an appetizer? I highly recommend the Rocky Mountain oysters."

That nearly made Logan wince. "I believe I'll pass on that one, Chuck."

"I second that," Hannah said. "A salad with vinaigrette would be good."

Chuck finally tore his gaze away from Hannah and centered it on Logan. "Can I bring you a salad, too, sir?"

No, but you can get the hell out of Dodge. "Just the coffee and a glass of water."

The waiter backed away from the table, then said, "I'll have that right out."

"What an idiot," Logan muttered after the guy disappeared into the kitchen.

Hannah frowned. "I thought he was very accommodating."

"He definitely wanted to accommodate you and it didn't have a damn thing to do with dinner." Hell, he sounded like a jealous lover.

Hannah looked understandably confused. "Excuse me?"

"You didn't notice the way he was looking at you?"

"He was just being friendly."

She apparently didn't realize her appeal when it came to the opposite sex, and he personally found that intriguing. "Look, I don't blame the guy. You're an extremely attractive woman, but for all he knows, we're a couple. The fact that he kept eyeing you wasn't appropriate in my book."

Her gaze momentarily wandered away and the color returned to her cheeks. "But we're not a couple, and he wasn't *eyeing* me."

"Believe me, he was." And he sure couldn't blame the guy when it came right down to it.

She picked up the cloth napkin near her right hand, unfolded it and laid it in her lap. "If he was, I didn't notice. Then again, I haven't been out much in the past few years."

"Since your…" If he kept going, he'd be treading on shaky ground. The kind that covered a major loss from the past. He knew that concept all too well.

She raised a brow. "Since my husband's death? It's okay. I've been able to talk about it without falling apart for the past four years."

He definitely admired her for that. Even after nine years, he hadn't been able to discuss his loss without flying into a rage. "I admire your resiliency," he said, all the while thinking he wished he had half of her tenacity.

Chuck picked that moment to bring the drinks and Hannah's salad. "Here you go, folks. Dinner will be right out."

As bad as Logan hated to admit it, he was actually glad to see the jerk, if only to grab the opportunity to turn to a lighter topic. "Thank you kindly, Chuck."

"You're welcome, sir."

After the waiter left the area, Logan returned his attention to Hannah. "So it's my understanding you recently obtained your degree."

She took a quick sip of water and sent him a proud smile. "Yes, I did, and apparently you've done your homework on me, too."

"I had to in order to locate you." Thanks to J. D. Lassiter not providing much information when they discovered the annuity's existence.

She picked up a fork and began moving lettuce around on the plate. "That old internet is a great resource for checking people out."

He only wished she would thoroughly check him out, and not on the computer. And where in the hell had *that* come from?

He cleared his throat and shifted slightly in his seat. "I take it you're satisfied I'm not some reprobate posing as an attorney."

"Yes, but frankly, I'm curious as to why you relocated from Dallas to Cheyenne, Wyoming. That must have been quite a culture shock."

He didn't want to delve into his reasons for leaving his former life behind. "Not that much of a shock. You find cowboys in both places."

"Were you a cowboy in another life, or just trying to blend in now?"

"I've ridden my share of horses, if that's what you mean."

She smiled again. "Let me guess. You were born into an affluent ranching family."

"Nope. A not-quite-poor farming family. Three generations, as a matter of fact. My parents ran a peach orchard in East Texas and raised a few cattle. They're semiretired now and disappointed I didn't stick around to take over the business."

"What made you decide to be a lawyer?"

He grinned. "When I wore overalls, people kept mistaking me for a plumber, and since clogged drains aren't my thing, studying the law made sense."

Her soft laughter traveled all the way to her striking green eyes. "Something tells me you're not going to let me live that one down."

Something told him he could wind up in hot water if he didn't stop viewing her as a desirable woman. "I'll let you off the hook, seeing as how we just met."

"And I will let you off the hook for not giving me fair warning before you showed up on my doorstep."

He still had those great images of her branded in his brain. "You know, I'm really glad I didn't decide to handle this over the phone. Otherwise, I wouldn't have met you, and something tells me I would have regretted that."

Hannah set down the fork, braced her elbow on the edge of the table and rested her cheek in her palm. "And I would have missed the opportunity to get all dressed up for a change and have a free meal."

She looked prettier than a painted picture come to life. Yep. Trouble with a capital *T* if he didn't get his mind back on business. "After you learn the details of your share of the Lassiter fortune, you'll be able to buy me dinner next time." Next time? Man, he was getting way ahead of himself, and that was totally out of character for his normally cautious self.

Hannah looked about as surprised as he felt over the comment. "That all depends on if I actually agree to accept my share, and that's doubtful."

He couldn't fathom anyone in their right mind turning down that much money. But before he had a chance to toss out an opinion, or the amount of the annuity held in her name, Chuck showed up with their entrées.

Logan ate his food with the gusto of a field hand, while Hannah basically picked at hers, the same way she had with the salad. By the time they were finished, and the plates were cleared, he had half a mind to invite her into the nearby bar to discuss business. But dark and cozy wouldn't help rein in his libido.

Hannah tossed her napkin aside and folded her hands before her. "Okay, we've put this off long enough. Tell me the details."

Logan took a drink of water in an attempt to rid the dryness in his throat. "The funds are currently in an annuity. You have the option to leave it as is and take payments. Or you can claim the lump sum. Your choice."

"How much?" she said after a few moments.

He noticed she looked a little flushed and decided retiring to the bar might not be a bad idea after all. "Maybe we should go into the lounge so you can have a drink before I continue."

Frustration showed in her expression. "I don't need a drink."

He'd begun to think he might. "Just a glass of wine to take the edge off."

She leaned forward and nailed him with a glare. "How *much?*"

"Five million dollars."

"I believe I will have that drink now."

Two

She'd never been much of a drinker, but at the moment Hannah sat on a sofa in the corner of a dimly lit bar, a vodka and tonic tightly gripped in her hand. "Five million dollars? Are you insane?"

Logan leaned back in the club chair and leveled his dark gaze on hers. "Hey, it's not my money. I'm only the messenger."

She set the glass down on the small table separating them, slid her fingers through the sides of her hair and resisted pulling it out by the roots. "You're saying that I can just sign some papers and you're going to hand me a fortune."

"It's a little more complicated than that."

After having the five-million-dollar bombshell dropped on her head, nothing seemed easy, including deciding to refuse it. "Would I have to go before some probate court?"

"No, but there are some stipulations."

She dropped her hands into her lap and sat back on the cushions. "Such as?"

"You have to sign a nondisclosure waiver in order to claim the inheritance."

"Nondisclosure?"

"That means if you take the money, by law you can't disclose your connection to the Lassiters to anyone."

She barked out a cynical laugh. "I refuse to do that. Not after living my entire life in the shadow of shame, thanks to my biological father's refusal to acknowledge me."

"Then you have reason to believe J. D. Lassiter is your father?"

Good reason. "Yes, there is a chance, but I don't know for certain because I have no real proof. Regardless, I do know I won't take a penny of his hush money."

Logan downed the last of his coffee, sat back on the opposing sofa and remained quiet a few moments. "What does your future hold in terms of your career?"

A little hardship, but nothing she couldn't handle. "I'm going to teach high-school human physiology and probably health classes as well."

He released a rough sigh. "It takes a lot of guts to stand in front of a room full of teenage boys and talk about the facts of life, especially looking the way you do."

Hannah appreciated his skill at doling out the compliments, even if she didn't understand it or quite believe it. "I assure you I can handle whatever teenage boys want to throw at me."

"I don't doubt that," he said. "But it's not going to be easy. I know because I was one once."

She imagined a very cute one at that. "Most men still retain some of those prepubescent qualities, don't you agree?"

He grinned, giving her another premiere dimple show. "Probably so. Do you have a job lined up?"

That caused her to glance away. "Not yet, but I've had my degree for less than two weeks, and that's when I immediately started the search. I expect to find something any day now."

"And if you don't?"

She'd harbored those same concerns due to the lack of prospects. "I'll manage fine, just as I've been managing since my husband died."

He sent her a sympathetic look. "That must have been a struggle, raising a child and going to school."

She'd been lucky enough to have help. Begrudging help. "My mother looked after my daughter when necessary until Cassie turned two. I lived off the settlement from my husband's work accident and that, coupled with Social Security benefits, allowed me to pay for day care and the bills while studying full-time. I obtained grants and student loans to finance my tuition."

"If you don't mind me asking, do you have any of the settlement left?"

She didn't exactly mind, but she felt certain she knew where he was heading—back into inheritance land. "Actually, the payments will end in October, so I still have six months."

He streaked a hand over the back of his neck. "You

do realize that if you accept this money, you'll be set for life. No worries financially for you or your daughter."

If Cassie's future played a role, she might reconsider taking the inheritance. "My daughter will be well provided for when she turns eighteen, thanks to my in-laws, who've established a million-dollar-plus trust fund in her name. Of course, I'm sure that will come with conditions, as those with fortunes exceeding the national debt are prone to do."

"Guess that explains your aversion to wealthy people."

Her aversion was limited to only the entitled wealthy, including Theresa and Marvin Armstrong. "Daniel's parents didn't exactly approve of my marriage to their son. Actually, they didn't approve of me. It was that whole illegitimate thing. They had no way of knowing if I had the appropriate breeding to contribute to the stellar Armstrong gene pool. Of course, when I became pregnant with Cassie, they had no say in the matter."

He seemed unaffected by her cynicism. "Are they involved in your daughter's life at all?"

"Theresa sends Cassie money on her birthday and collector dolls at Christmas that carry instructions not to remove them from the box so they'll retain their value. What good is a doll you can't play with?"

"Have they ever seen her?"

"Only once." And once had been quite enough. "When Cassie was two, they flew us out to North Carolina for a visit. It didn't take long to realize that my mother-in-law and active toddlers don't mix. After Theresa accused me of raising a wild animal, I told her

I'd find a good kennel where I could board Cassie next time. Fortunately, there wasn't a next time."

Logan released a deep, sexy laugh. "You're hell on wheels, aren't you?"

She took another sip of the cocktail to clear the bitter taste in her mouth. "After growing up a poor fatherless child, I learned to be. Also, my mother was extremely unsocial and rather unhappy over raising a daughter alone, to say the least. I took an opposite path and made it my goal to be upbeat and sociable."

He grinned. "I bet you were a cheerleader."

She returned his smile. "Yes, I was, and I could do a mean backflip."

"Think you could still do it?"

"I don't know. It's been a while, but I suppose I could don my cheerleading skirt, though it's probably a little tight, and give it the old college try."

He winked, sending a succession of pleasant chills down Hannah's body. "I'd like to see that."

"If you're like most men, you just want to see up my skirt." Had she really said that?

He sent her a sly grin. "I do admire limber women."

A brief span of silence passed, a few indefinable moments following unmistakable innuendo. Hannah couldn't recall the last time she'd actually flirted with someone aside from her husband. And she'd been flirting with a virtual stranger. An extremely handsome, successful stranger.

A very young, very peppy blonde waitress sauntered over and flashed a grin. "Can I get you anything, sir?"

"Bring me a cola," Logan said without cracking a smile.

She glanced at Hannah. "What about you, ma'am?"

"No, thank you."

"Are you sure?" Logan asked. "You wouldn't like one more round?"

She was sorely tempted, but too sensible to give in. "I'm driving, remember?"

"I could drive you home if you change your mind."

"That would be too much trouble," she said, knowing that if he came anywhere near her empty house, she might make a colossal mistake.

"It's not a problem."

It could be if she didn't proceed with caution. "I'm fine for now. But thanks."

Once the waitress left, Hannah opted for a subject change. "Now that you know quite a bit about me, what about you?"

He pushed his empty coffee cup aside. "What do you want to know?"

Plenty. "I saw on your profile you're single. Have you ever been married?"

His expression went suddenly somber. "Once. I've been divorced for eight years."

She couldn't imagine a man of his caliber remaining unattached all that time. "Any relationships since?"

"Nothing serious."

She tapped her chin and pretended to think. "Let me guess. You have a woman in every court."

His smile returned, but only halfway. "Not even close. I work a lot of hours so I don't have much time for a social life."

"Did you take a vow of celibacy?" Heaven help her, the vodka had completely destroyed her verbal filter.

When the waitress returned with the cola, Logan pulled out his wallet and handed her a platinum card to close out the tab, or so Hannah assumed. "Keep it open for the time being," he said, shattering her assumptions.

Once the waitress retreated, Hannah attempted to backtrack. "Forget I asked that last question. It's really none of my business."

"It's okay," he said. "I've had a few relationships based solely on convenience. What about you?"

He'd presented a good case of turnabout being fair play, but she simply had little to tell when it came to the dating game. "Like you, I haven't had time to seriously consider the social scene. I have had a couple of coffee dates in the past year, but they were disastrous. One guy still lived at his mother's house in the basement, and the other's only goal was to stay in school as long as possible. He already had three graduate degrees."

"Apparently the last guy was fairly smart," he said.

"True, but both made it quite clear they weren't particularly fond of children, and that's a deal breaker. Not to mention I'm not going to subject my child to a man unless he's earned my trust."

He traced the rim of the glass with his thumb. "It's logical that you would have major concerns in that department."

"Very true. And I have to admit I'm fairly protective of her. Some might even say overprotective." Including her best friend, Gina.

Logan downed the last of his drink and set it aside. "I'm not sure there is such a thing in this day and time."

"But I've been known to take it to extremes. I've even considered encasing her in bubble wrap every day before I send her off to school."

Her attempt at humor seemed to fall flat for Logan.

"You really can't protect them from everything, and that's a damn shame."

His solemn tone spurred Hannah's curiosity. "Do you have children from your previous marriage?"

He momentarily looked away. "No."

Definitely a story there. "Was that a mutual decision between you and your wife?" Realizing she'd become the ultimate Nosy Nellie, she raised her hands, palms forward. "I'm so sorry. I'm not normally this intrusive."

"My wife was an attorney, too," he continued, as if her prying didn't bother him. "Having kids wasn't in the cards for us, and that was probably just as well."

"How long were you married?"

"A little over seven years."

She started to ask if he'd been plagued with the legendary itch but didn't want to destroy her honorable-man image. "I'm sorry to hear that. I'm sure the divorce process can be tough."

"Ours was pretty contentious. But it wasn't anything compared to losing someone to death."

He almost sounded as if he'd had experience with that as well. "They're both losses, and they both require navigating the grief process. I was somewhat lucky in that respect. I had Cassie to see me through the rough times."

"How old was she when your husband died?" he asked.

"I was five months pregnant, so he never saw her." She was somewhat amazed she'd gotten through that revelation without falling apart. Maybe her grief cycle was finally nearing completion.

"At least you were left with a part of him," Logan

said gruffly. "I assume that did provide some conso-lation."

A good-looking and intuitive man, a rare combina-tion in Hannah's limited experience. "I'm very sur-prised by your accurate perception, Mr. Whittaker. Most of the time people look at me with pity when they learn the details. I appreciate their sympathy, but I'm not a lost cause."

"It's Logan," he told her. "And you're not remotely a lost cause or someone who deserves pity. You de-serve respect and congratulations for moving on with your life, Hannah."

Somewhat self-conscious over the compliment, and oddly excited over hearing her name on his lips, she began to fold the corner of the cocktail napkin back and forth. "Believe me, the first two years weren't pretty. I cried a lot and I had a few serious bouts of self-pity. But then Cassie would reach a milestone, like her first steps and the first time she said 'Mama,' and I real-ized I had to be strong for her. I began to look at every day as a chance for new opportunities. A new begin-ning, so to speak."

The waitress came back to the table and eyed Han-nah's empty glass. "Sure I can't get you another?"

She glanced at the clock hanging over the bar and after noticing it was nearly 10:00 p.m., she couldn't believe how quickly the time had flown by. "Actually, it's getting late. I should probably be going."

"It's not that late," Logan said. "Like I told you be-fore, I'll make sure you get home safely if you want to live a little and have another vodka and tonic."

Hannah mulled over the offer for a few moments. Her daughter was at a sleepover, she had no desire to watch TV, and she was in the company of a very attractive and attentive man who promised to keep her safe. What would be the harm in having one more drink?

"I should never have ordered that second drink."

Logan regarded Hannah across the truck's cab as he pulled to a stop at the curb near her driveway. "It's my fault for encouraging you."

She lifted her face from her hands and attempted a smile. "You didn't force me at gunpoint. And you had no idea I'm such a lightweight when it comes to alcohol."

Funny, she seemed perfectly coherent to him, both back in the bar and now. "Are you feeling okay?"

"Just a little fuzzy and worried about my car. It's not much, but it's all that I have."

He'd noticed the sedan had seen better days. "It's been secured in the valet garage, and I'll make certain it's delivered to you first thing in the morning."

"You've done too much already," she said. "I really could have called a cab."

In reality, he hadn't been ready to say good-night, although he couldn't quite understand why. Or maybe he understood it and didn't want to admit it. "Like I told you, it's not a problem. You don't know who you can trust these days, especially when you're an attractive woman."

She gave him a winning grin. "I bet you say that to all the women who refuse a five-million-dollar inheritance."

"You happen to be the first in that regard." Absolutely the first woman in a long, long time to completely capture his interest on a first meeting. A business meeting to boot. "I'm hoping you haven't totally ruled out taking the money."

"Yes, I have. I know you probably think I've lost my mind, but I do have my reasons."

Yeah, and he'd figured them out—she was refusing on the basis of principle. He sure as hell didn't see that often in his line of work. "Well, I'm not going to pressure you, but I will check back with you tomorrow after you've slept on it."

She blinked and hid a yawn behind her hand. "Speaking of sleeping, I'm suddenly very tired. I guess it's time to bid you adieu."

When Hannah reached for the door handle, Logan touched her arm to gain her attention. "I'll get that for you."

"Whaddya know," she said. "Looks like chivalry is still alive and well after all." She followed the comment with a soft, breathless laugh that sent his imagination into overdrive.

Before he acted on impulse, Logan quickly slid out of the driver's seat, rounded the hood and opened the door for Hannah. She had a little trouble climbing out, which led him to take her hand to assist her. Weird thing was, he didn't exactly want to let go of her hand, but he did, with effort.

He followed behind her as they traveled the path to the entry, trying hard to keep his gaze focused on that silky auburn hair that swayed slightly with each step she took, not her butt that did a little swaying, too.

Right before they reached the front porch, Hannah glanced back and smiled. "At least I'm not falling-down drunk." Then she immediately tripped on the first step.

Logan caught her elbow before she landed on that butt he'd been trying to ignore. "Careful."

"I'm just clumsy," she said as he guided her up the remaining steps.

Once they reached the door, he released her arm and she sent him another sleepy smile. "I really enjoyed the evening, Logan. And if you'll just send me what I need to sign to relinquish the money, I'll mail it back to you immediately."

He still wasn't convinced she was doing the right thing in that regard. "We'll talk about that later. Right now getting you to bed is more important." Dammit, that sounded like a freaking proposition.

"Do you want to come in?" she asked, taking him totally by surprise.

"I don't think that's a good idea." Actually, it sounded like a great idea, but he was too keyed up to honestly believe he could control his libido.

She clutched her bag to her chest. "Oh, I get it. You're afraid you're going to be accosted by the poor, single mom who hasn't had sex in almost seven years."

Oh, hell. "That's not it at all. I just respect you enough not to put us in the position where we might do something we regret, because, lady, being alone with you could lead to all sorts of things."

She leaned a shoulder against the support column and inclined her head. "Really?"

"Really. In case you haven't noticed, I've had a hard time keeping my eyes off you tonight." He was having a real *hard* time right now.

She barked out a laugh. "I'm sorry, but I'm having a difficult time believing you would be interested in me."

She couldn't be more wrong. "Why wouldn't I be?

You're smart and savvy and pretty damn brave to raise a child on your own and finish college at the same time."

"Keep going."

He could…all night. "You're a survivor and very beautiful, although you don't seem to know that. And that's not only hard to find in a beautiful woman, it's appealing."

"And?"

"Right now I'd like to kiss you," he blurted out before his brain caught up with his mouth. "But I'm not going to."

"Why not?" she asked, looking thoroughly disappointed.

"Because if I kissed you, I might not want to stop there. And as I've said, I respect you too much to—"

Hannah cut off his words by circling one hand around his neck and landing her lips on his, giving him the kiss he'd been halfheartedly trying to avoid.

Logan was mildly aware she'd dropped her purse, and very aware she kissed him like she hadn't been kissed in a long, long time—with the soft glide of her tongue against his, bringing on a strong stirring south of his belt buckle. He grazed his hand up her side until his palm rested close to her breast, and he heard her breath catch as she moved flush against him. He considered telling her they should take it inside the house before someone called the cops, but then she pulled abruptly away from him and took a step back.

Hannah touched her fingertips to her lips, her face flushed, her emerald eyes wide with shock. "I cannot believe I just did that. And I can't imagine what you must be thinking about me right now."

He was thinking he wanted her. Badly. "Hey, it's chemistry. It happens. Couple that with a few cocktails—"

"And you get some thirty-year-old woman acting totally foolish."

He tucked a strand of hair behind her ear. "You don't have to feel foolish or ashamed, Hannah. I'm personally flattered that you kissed me."

She snatched her bag from the cement floor and hugged it tightly again. "I didn't give you a whole lot of choice."

"You only did what I wanted to do." Trouble was, he wanted to do it again, and more. "For the record, I think you're one helluva sexy woman and I'd really like to get to know you better."

"But we've just met," she said. "We don't really know anything about each other."

He knew enough to want to move forward and see where it might lead. "That's the get-to-know-each-other-better part."

"We don't live in the same town."

"True, but it's only a ninety-mile drive."

"You're busy and I have a five-year-old child who is currently in school, plus I'm looking for a job."

He remembered another search she should be conducting, and this could be the key to spending more time with her. "There's something I've been meaning to ask you all night."

"Have I taken total leave of my senses?"

He appreciated her wit, too. "This is about your biological father."

That seemed to sober her up. "What about him?"

"Just wondering if you have any details about his life."

She sighed. "I only know that my mother hooked up with some guy who left her high and dry when she became pregnant with me. According to her, he was both ruthless and worthless."

Some people might describe J. D. Lassiter that way. "Did she ever offer to give you a name?"

"No, and I didn't ask. I figured that if he wanted nothing to do with me, then I wanted nothing to do with him." Her tone was laced with false bravado.

He did have a hard time believing J.D. would be so cold and uncaring that he would ignore his own flesh and blood no matter what the circumstances. "Maybe there were underlying issues that prevented him from being involved in your life."

"Do you mean the part about him being an absolute bastard, or that he was married?"

Finally, a little more to go on. "Do you know that to be a fact? The married part."

"My mother hinted at that, but again, I can't be certain."

"Then maybe it's time you try to find out the truth. You owe it to yourself and to your daughter. Because if J.D. is actually your father, you have siblings."

Hannah seemed to mull that over for a time before she spoke again. "How do you propose I do that?"

"With my help."

She frowned. "Why would you even want to help me?"

"Because I can't imagine what it would be like to have more questions than answers." In some ways he did know that. Intimately. "And since I'm an attorney, and I know the Lassiters personally, I could do some subtle investigating without looking suspicious."

"It seems to me you would be too busy to take this on."

"Actually, I have a light caseload this week." Or he would as soon as he asked his assistant to postpone a few follow-up appointments. "But I would definitely want you to be actively involved in the search."

"How do you suggest I do that from here?"

Here came the part that would probably have her questioning his motives. "Not here. In Cheyenne. You could stay with me for a few days and I'll show you the sights and introduce you to a few people. You could so some research during the day while I'm at work."

Hannah's mouth opened slightly before she snapped it shut. "Stay with you?"

He definitely understood why that part of the plan might get her hackles up. "Look, I have a forty-five-hundred-square-foot house with five bedrooms and seven baths. You'd have your own space. In fact, the master bedroom is downstairs and the guest rooms are all upstairs. We could go for days and not even see each other." Like he intended for that to happen.

"Good heavens, why would a confirmed bachelor need a house that size?"

"I got a good deal on the place when the couple had to transfer out of state. And I like to entertain."

"Do you have a harem?"

He couldn't help but laugh for the second time tonight, something he'd rarely done over the past few years. "No harem. But I have five acres and a couple of horses, as well as a gourmet kitchen. My housekeeper comes by twice a week and makes meals in advance if I don't want to cook."

"You know how to cook?" she asked, sounding doubtful.

"Yeah. I know my way around the stove."

She smiled. "Mac and cheese? BLT sandwiches? Or maybe when you're feeling adventurous, you actually tackle scrambled eggs?"

"My favorite adventurous meal will always be Italian. You'd like my mostaccioli."

She loosened her grip on her bag and slipped the strap on her shoulder. "As tempting as that sounds, I can't just take off for Cheyenne without my daughter. She won't be out of school for five weeks."

"Is there someone who could watch her for a few days?" Damn, he almost sounded desperate.

"Possibly, but I've never left Cassie alone for more than a night," she said. "I don't know how she would handle it. I don't know how *I* would handle it. Besides, I'm not sure I could accomplish that much in a few days even if I did decide to go."

He might be losing the battle, but he intended to win the war. "You could drive up for day trips, but that would require a lot of driving. If you stayed with me a couple of days, that would give us time to get to know each other better."

"Residing in a stranger's house would require a huge leap of faith."

He closed the space between them and cupped her face in his palm. "We're not strangers anymore. Not after you did this."

He kissed her softly, thoroughly, with just enough exploration to tempt her to take him up on his offer.

And once he was done, he moved away but kept his gaze locked on hers. "There could be more of that if you decide you want it. Again, no pressure. I'm just asking you to think about it. You might have the answers you need about your heritage, and we might find out we enjoy each other's company. Unless you're afraid to explore the possibilities..."

Logan realized he'd hit a home run when he saw a hint of defiance in Hannah's eyes. "I'm not the cowardly type, but I am cautious because I have to be. However, I will consider your suggestion and give you my answer tomorrow."

"Do you mind giving me your number? So I can call and let you know when your car's on its way." And in case he needed to further plead his case.

She dug through her purse for a pen and paper and scribbled down the information on the back of a receipt. "That's my home and cell number," she said as she handed it over. "Feel free to send me a text."

As Logan pocketed the paper, Hannah withdrew her keys, turned around and unlocked the door with a little effort, then walked inside without another word.

Logan was left alone on the porch to ponder why being with her again seemed so damn important. He had his choice of beautiful women back in Cheyenne, although most hadn't come close to capturing his interest like Hannah Armstrong.

He could chalk it up to chemistry, but he inherently knew that was only part of it. He did appreciate her keen sense of humor, knock-'em-dead body and those expressive green eyes that could drop a man in his tracks. He appreciated her all-fire independence and that she had the temperament of a mother bear when it came to her kid. In some ways, that attracted him more than anything else. But above all, she'd experienced the loss of a loved one. Their true common ground.

Hannah might understand his grief because she'd lived it, but if he told her his story, would she see him in the same light? Or would she turn away when she learned the truth?

Only time would tell if he'd find the courage to confess his greatest sin—he'd been partially to blame for the death of his only child.

Three

Her car was back, and so was the man who'd been foremost on her mind all morning long. All night, too.

Hannah peered out the window and watched Logan emerge from her aged blue sedan dressed in a long-sleeved black shirt, faded jeans secured by a belt with a shiny buckle and dark boots. Her heart immediately went on a marathon, the direct effect of an undeniable attraction she'd experienced all too well last night. That attraction had given her the courage to kiss him, something she normally wouldn't have the audacity to do. But by golly she had, and she'd liked it. A lot.

Hormones. That had to be it. Those pesky freaks of nature that made people act on impulse. She made a point to banish them as soon as she climbed out of bed. Granted, when he'd called to say he was bringing the car back, she'd made certain she looked more presentable than she had during their first meeting. She'd dressed in simple, understated clothing—white capri pants, light green, short-sleeved shirt and rhinestone-embellished flip-flops. Of course, she had put on a little makeup and pulled her hair back in a sleek, low ponytail. The silver hoop earrings might be a little much, but it was too late to take them off unless she ripped them out of her earlobes.

When the bell rang, Hannah automatically smoothed her palms over the sides of her hair and the front of the blouse. She measured her steps to avoid looking too eager, even though she wanted to hurl herself onto the porch and launch into his arms. Instead, she gave herself a mental pep talk on the virtues of subtlety before she slowly opened the door.

He greeted her with a dimpled grin and surprisingly stuck out his hand. "Mornin'. I'm Logan Whittaker, in case you've forgotten."

Hannah didn't know whether to kick him in the shin or kiss that sexy look off his face. She chose option three—play along for now—and accepted his offered handshake. She noticed the calluses and the width of his palm as he gave her hand a slight squeeze before he released her. "Good morning, Mr. Whittaker, and thank you for returning my car."

"You're welcome, but after last night, you should call me Logan."

Cue the blush. "I'm trying to forget about last night."

"Good luck with that because I sure can't forget it. In fact, it kept me tossing and turning most of the night."

She'd experienced the same restlessness, not that she'd admit it to him. "Do I need to drive you back to the lodge?"

"Nope," he said. "One of the valet guys will be here in about ten minutes."

Must be nice to have people at your beck and call, but she supposed that perk came with money. "Are you sure I can't drop you off? It's the least I can do."

"I'm sure, but I'm not leaving until we discuss your inheritance and my proposal."

No amount of money would ever convince her to agree to sign a nondisclosure form, even if she had no intention of aligning herself with the Lassiters. And that's the way it would stay. "I haven't changed my mind about the money, and the jury's still out on the other, to coin a legal phrase."

"Well, since you haven't ruled it out, I think you should let me in to argue my case. I'm housebroken and I won't destroy the furniture."

The sexy dog. "I suppose that's okay, but I have to warn you, the place is a mess, thanks to my child and the plumbing problems."

He had the gall to grin again, revealing those damnable dimples and perfectly straight, white teeth. "I promise you won't regret hearing me out."

She already did when he brushed past her and she caught the subtle scent of his cologne. Even more when once they moved inside, he turned and asked, "Where do you want me?"

An unexpected barrage of questionable images assaulted Hannah, sending her mind in the direction of unadvisable possibilities. Clearly those inherent female desires she'd tried to bury in everyday life weren't completely dead. That was okay, as long as she didn't act on them. Again.

She swallowed hard and bumped the door closed

with her bottom. "Let's go in the dining room." A safe place to interact with Mr. Charisma. "Actually, the floor's wet in there, so we can stay in here." First, she had to clear the worn floral couch of kid debris.

Before she could do that, Logan presented a frown that didn't detract from his good looks one iota. "Leaky pipe?"

"You could definitely say that. I managed to cut off the water under the sink, but this morning I got up only to discover the valve is leaking, too. Now the flood waters are trying to take over my kitchen."

"Tough break."

When Logan began rolling up his sleeves, Hannah's mouth dropped open. "What are you doing?"

"I'm pretty handy when it comes to pipe problems."

"That's not what you said yesterday."

"I've learned not to reveal my skills. Otherwise I'll be hounded every time someone has a plumbing issue. But for you, I'm willing to take a look."

She'd already taken a look. A covert look at his toned forearms threaded with veins, and the opening in his collar that revealed tanned skin and a slight shading of hair she'd tried not to notice last night. "Now I get it. You're really a repressed plumber masquerading as a lawyer."

His reappearing smile had the impact of a jackhammer. "No, but I am good with my hands."

She'd bet her last buck on that. "Thanks for offering to help, but it's not necessary. A real plumber should be here today."

Now he looked plain cynical. "Good luck with that, too. They don't get in a big hurry on a Saturday." He winked. "Besides, I'll save you that weekend rate and check it out for free."

He did have a valid argument, and she really liked the free part. What would be the harm in letting him peruse her pipes, or anything else of hers he'd like to peruse? She seriously needed to get a hold on her self-control. "Fine, but you're going to get wet. I did."

"Not a problem. Getting wet isn't always a bad thing."

Logan's suggestive tone wasn't lost on her. "Since you insist, be my guest." She pointed toward the opening to the dining room. "Just swim through there and keep going. You can't miss the kitchen sink."

Hannah followed behind Logan, covertly sizing up his butt on the way. A really nice butt, not that she was surprised. He happened to be one major male specimen, and she'd have to be in a coma not to notice. Still, she refused to let a sexy, dark-eyed, dimpled cowboy attorney muddle her mind. She'd let him fix her sink and say his piece before sending him packing back to Cheyenne without her.

Logan grabbed a wrench from the counter, lowered to his knees and stuck his head into the cabinet beneath the sink. Hannah leaned back against the counter to watch, unable to suppress a laugh over the string of oaths coming out of the lawyer's mouth.

"Sorry," he muttered without looking back. "I need to tighten a fitting and it's not cooperating."

"Is that the reason for the leak?"

"Yeah. It's a little corroded and probably should be replaced eventually. But I think I can get it to hold."

At least that would save her an after-business-hours service call. "That's a relief."

"Don't be relieved until I say it's repaired."

A few minutes passed, filled with a little more cursing and the occasional groan, until Logan finally emerged from beneath the cabinet and turned on the sink. Seemingly satisfied, he set the wrench aside and sent Hannah another devastating smile. "All done for the time being. Again, it needs to be replaced. Actually, all the pipes should be replaced."

Hannah sighed. "So I've been told. The house was built over forty years ago and it's systematically falling apart. I just paid for a new furnace. That pretty much ate up my reserves and blew my budget."

He wiped his hands on the towel beside the sink. "If you claim the inheritance, you'd never have to worry about a tight budget."

She couldn't deny the concept appealed to her greatly, but the cost to her principles was simply too high. "As I've said, I have no intention of taking my share." Even if J. D. Lassiter did owe her that much. But money could never make up for the years she'd spent in a constant state of wondering where she had come from.

Logan leaned back against the counter opposite Hannah. "And what *are* your intentions when it comes to my invitation?"

"I just don't see the wisdom in running off to Cheyenne on what will probably be a wild-goose chase."

"But it might not be at all. And you would also have the opportunity to meet some of the Lassiters, in case you decide you'd like to connect with your relatives since you wouldn't be bound by the nondisclosure."

"I'm not interested in connecting with the Lassiters."

He studied her for a few moments, questions in his eyes. "Aside from your in-laws, do you have any family?"

Hannah shook her head. "No. I'm an only child and so was my mother. My grandparents have been gone for many years."

"Then wouldn't it be good to get to know the family you never knew existed?" he asked.

She shrugged. "I've gone all these years without knowing, so I'm sure I'll survive if I never meet them."

"What about your daughter? Don't you think she deserves to know she has another family?"

The sound of rapid footsteps signaled the arrival of said daughter. Hannah's attention turned to her right to see the feisty five-year-old twirling through the dining area wearing a pink boa and matching tutu that covered her aqua shirt and shorts, with a fake diamond tiara planted atop her head. She waved around the star wand that she gripped in her fist and shouted, "I'm queen of the frog fairies!"

Cassie stopped turning circles when she spotted the strange man in the kitchen, yet she didn't stop her forward progress. Instead, she charged up to Logan, where she paused to give him a partially toothless grin. "Are you a frog or a prince?"

Possibly a toad in prince clothing, Hannah decided, but that remained to be seen. "This is Mr. Whittaker, Cassie, and he's a lawyer. Do you know what that is, sweetie?"

Her daughter glanced back and rolled her eyes. "I'm not a baby, Mama. I'm almost six and I watch the law shows on TV with Shelly. That's how I learned about lawyers. They look mad all the time and yell 'I object.'"

Hannah made a mental note to have a long talk with the sitter about appropriate television programs for a kindergartner. When Cassie began twirling again, she caught her daughter by the shoulders and turned her to face Logan. "What do you say to Mr. Whittaker?"

Cassie curtsied and grinned. "It's nice to meet you, Mr. Whittaker."

Logan attempted a smile but it didn't make its way to his eyes. In fact, he almost looked sad. "It's nice to meet you, too, Your Highness."

Being addressed as royalty seemed to please Cassie greatly. "Do you have a little girl?"

His gaze wandered away for a moment before he returned it to Cassie. "No, I don't."

"A little boy?" Cassie topped off the comment with a sour look.

"Nope. No kids."

Hannah sensed Logan's discomfort and chalked it up to someone who hadn't been around children, and maybe didn't care to be around them. "Now that the introductions are over, go pick up your toys, Cassandra Jane, and start deciding what you'll be wearing to school on Monday since that takes you at least two days."

That statement earned a frown from her daughter. "Can I just wear this?"

"I think you should save that outfit for playtime. Now scoot."

Cassie backed toward the dining room, keeping her smile trained on Logan. "I think you're a prince," she said, then turned and sprinted away.

Once her daughter had vacated the premises, Hannah returned her attention to Logan. "I'm sorry. She's really into fairy tales these days, and she doesn't seem to know a stranger. Frankly, that worries me sometimes. I'm afraid someday she'll encounter someone with questionable intentions. I've cautioned her time and again, but I'm not sure she understands the risk in that behavior."

"I understand why that would worry you," he said. "But I guess you have to trust that she'll remember your warnings if the situation presents itself."

Hannah sighed. "I hope so. She's everything to me and sometimes I'd like to keep her locked in her room until she's eighteen."

He grinned. "Encased in bubble wrap, right?"

She was pleasantly surprised he remembered that from the night before. "Bubble wrap with rhinestones. Now what were you saying before we were interrupted by the queen?"

"Mama! Where's my purple shorts?"

Hannah gritted her teeth and spoke through them. "Just a minute, Cassie."

"Look, maybe this isn't a good time to discuss this...." Logan said.

She was beginning to wonder that same thing. "You're probably right. And it's probably best if I say thanks, but no thanks, to your proposal, although I sincerely appreciate your offer."

When Logan's phone beeped, he took the cell out of his back pocket and swiped the screen. "The driver's here."

"Then I guess you better go." She sounded disappointed, even to her own ears.

He pocketed his wallet then unrolled his sleeves. "Do you have a pen and paper handy so I can give you my info?"

Hannah withdrew a pencil from the tin container on the counter and tore a piece of paper from the nearby notepad. "Here you go, but don't forget, I already have your card."

He turned his back and began jotting something down. "Yeah, but you don't have my home address."

She swallowed hard. "Why would I need that?"

He faced her again, caught her hand and placed the card in her palm. "In case you change your mind and decide to spend a few days as my guest in Cheyenne."

Oh, how tempting that would be. But... "I would have to ask my friend Gina if Cassie could stay with her. And I'd have to suspend my job search, even though that's not going anywhere right now." Funny, she sounded as if she was actually considering it.

He took a brief look around before he leaned over and brushed a kiss across her lips. "If you do decide to come, don't worry about calling. Just surprise me and show up."

With that, he strode through the living room and out the door, leaving Hannah standing in the kitchen in a semi-stupor until reality finally set in. Then she snatched up the cordless phone and pounded out a number on her way to the bedroom, where she closed the door. As soon as she heard the familiar hello, she said the only thing she could think to say.

"Help!"

"He wants you to do *what*?"

Sitting in a high-back stool at the granite island in her best friend's kitchen, Hannah was taken aback by Gina Romero's strong reaction to her declaration. Normally the woman rode her mercilessly about finding a man. "I'll speak more slowly this time. He wants me to go to Cheyenne for a few days and investigate the possibility that the man I'm inheriting from might be my biological father." She sure as heck wasn't going to reveal that inheritance was basically a fortune.

Gina swept one hand through her bobbed blond hair and narrowed her blue eyes. "Is that all he wants to investigate?"

Hannah would swear her face had morphed into a furnace. "Don't be ridiculous, Gina."

"Don't be naive, Hannah."

"I'm not being naive." Even if she wasn't being completely truthful. "He really is trying to help me."

Gina handed her eight-month-old son, Trey, another cracker when he began to squirm in the nearby high chair. "So tell me what's so special about this mystery attorney who wants to *help* you."

That could take hours. "Well, he's fairly tall, has dark hair and light brown eyes. Oh, and he has incredible dimples."

Gina gave her a good eye-rolling, the second Hannah had received today. "Okay. So he's a hunk, but does he have anything else to back that up?"

"As a matter of fact, he does. He's a full partner in a very prestigious law firm in Cheyenne."

"How's his butt?" she asked in a conspiratorial whisper.

The memory brought about Hannah's smile. "Stellar."

"Well, then, why aren't you home packing?"

"You'd think that would be enough, but I still have quite a few reservations."

"Unless you're lying and he's really in his eighties and drives a Studebaker, you should go for it."

"He's thirty-eight and drives a Mercedes. But he's also childless and divorced."

"Not everyone who's divorced is an ogre, Hannah," Gina said. "You can't judge him by your experience with that Henry what's-his-name you went out with for a while."

Gina could have gone all year without mentioning that jerk. "I only went out with him twice. But you know I worry when I meet a man who couldn't make his marriage work."

Gina frowned. "There are all sorts of reasons why marriages don't work, and it might not have even been his fault."

She couldn't argue that point since she had no details about Logan's divorce. "But what if it was his fault? What if he has some horrible habits that can't be overlooked?" Or worse, what if he cheated on his wife?

When the baby began to fuss, Gina rifled through the box of crackers and handed another one to her son. "Tell me, did this attorney do anything weird at dinner like that Henry guy you dated? Did he pick his teeth and belch? Or did he try to unsnap your bra when you hugged him good-night?"

"I didn't hug him good-night."

"Too bad."

"But I did kiss him."

Gina slapped her palm on the table, sending the baby into a fit of giggles. "You've been sitting here for ten minutes and you're just now telling me this?"

"It was a mistake." A huge one. "I had a couple of drinks and I guess it stripped me of all my inhibitions."

Gina sent her a sly look. "Question is, did you strip following the kiss?"

Heaven forbid. "Of course not. I just met the guy and I'm not that stupid."

"Yet you're considering going away with him," Gina said, adding a suspicious stare.

"I wouldn't be going away with him. I'd be staying at his house, which is very big, according to Logan."

"Wonder if his house is the only thing that's big."

Hannah playfully slapped at Gina's arm. "Stop it. This has to do with filling in the missing pieces of my family history, not getting friendly with Logan."

"Sure it does, Hannah. Just keep telling yourself that and you might start to believe it."

Leave it to Gina to see right through her ruse. "So what if I am attracted to him? Is there anything wrong with that?"

Gina made a one-handed catch of Trey's cracker when he tossed it at her. "There's absolutely nothing wrong with that. In fact, it's about time you start living again, girlfriend."

Same song, fiftieth verse. "I have been living, *girl-friend.* I've finished school and raised my daughter and I'm about to start a new career."

"Don't forget you cared for your ungrateful mother during the final months of her illness." Gina reached across the island and laid a palm on Hannah's forearm. "What you've done for your family since Danny's death is admirable. Heck, I'm not sure I could do the same thing if something happened to Frank. But now you need to do something for yourself."

Hannah still harbored several concerns. "What if I make this trip, decide that he's someone I want to spend a lot more time with and end up getting hurt?"

"That will happen only if you let him hurt you."

"True, but you have no idea how I felt being around him last night. I could barely think."

"Chemistry will cloud your mind every time."

Chemistry she could handle. "I'm worried it's more than that, Gina. I wish I could explain it." How could she when she couldn't explain it to herself? "I sense he really is a compassionate person, and maybe he's had some hard times during his life, too."

Gina took Trey from the high chair, placed him in the playpen and then signaled Hannah to join her in the adjacent den. She sat on the sofa and patted the space beside her. "Come here and let's have a heart-to-heart."

Hannah claimed her spot on the couch and prepared for a friendly lecture. "Bestow me with your sage advice, oh, wise one."

Gina sent her a smile. "Look, while we were growing up, you always walked the straight and narrow, always striving to be the best cheerleader, best student and an all-around good girl."

She bristled over her friend's words. "And what was wrong with that?"

"Because you did all those things to please your mother, and it never seemed to matter. Then you married Danny at the ripe old age of twenty. You worked hard to please him by quitting college so he could go to trade school when his parents cut him off because he married you."

She could feel her blood pressure begin to rise. "I loved Danny with all my heart and he loved me."

"Yes, he did, and he appreciated your efforts, unlike Ruth. But don't you think it's time you have a little adventure?"

Adventure had been a word sorely missing from

her vocabulary. "Maybe you're right, but what do I do about Cassie?"

Gina looked at her as if she'd lost her mind. "I can't count the times you've kept Michaela when Frank and I went out of town for a long weekend, including the one when I got pregnant with Trey. It's way past time for me to return the favor and watch Cassie for however long it takes for you to thoroughly investigate the attorney."

Hannah couldn't stop the flow of sexy, forbidden thoughts streaming through her imagination, until reality came calling once more. "But you're going to be saddled with two giggling girls and a baby. That doesn't seem fair."

Gina stood and began picking up the toys bouncing across the hardwood floors while Trey kept hurling more over the side of the playpen. "I'm used to this little guy's antics, and the girls will be in school during the day. Unless you plan to be gone until they reach puberty, it shouldn't be a problem."

"If I do go—" and that was a major *if* "—I only plan to stay a couple of days. A week, tops. But you're still going to have to deal with them at night, not to mention you have a husband to care for and—"

Gina held up a finger to silence her. "Frank has been trained well. And besides, he's been talking about trying for another kid next year. I might as well get in some practice before he knocks me up a third time."

The sound of those giggling girls grew closer and reached a crescendo as one red-headed ball of fire and one petite, brown-haired follower rushed into the room dressed in too-big formal attire, their faces showing the signs of a makeup attack.

"Aren't we pretty, Mama?" Cassie asked as she spun around in the red sequined strapless gown.

"Very," Hannah lied when she caught sight of the charcoal smudges outlining her daughter's eyes. "But did you have permission to raid Gina's closet?"

"Those came out of my cedar chest, Hannah," Gina said. "Cassie's wearing my prom dress and Michaela's wearing yours, in case you didn't recognize it."

Hannah did recognize the black silk gown all right, but she didn't remember giving it to her friend. "What are you doing with it?"

Gina looked somewhat chagrined. "I borrowed it and forgot to give it back."

Michaela's grin looked as lopsided as her high ponytail, thanks to the scarlet lipstick running askew from her mouth. "Can I keep it, Hannah?"

"Yes, honey, you most certainly can." The terrible memories of her part-octopus prom date, Ryan, were still attached to the gown, so no great loss.

"Do you have something you'd like to ask your daughter, Hannah?" Gina inquired.

Hannah supposed it wouldn't hurt to get Cassie's reaction to the possibility of her traveling to Cheyenne. "Sweetie, if I decided to take a trip out of town for a few days, would you mind staying here with Michaela and Gina?"

Cassie ran right out of her oversized high heels and practically tackled Hannah with a voracious hug. "I want to stay, Mama! When are you going?"

Good question. She pulled Cassie into her lap and planted a kiss on her makeup-caked cheek. "I'm not sure yet. Maybe tonight, but probably tomorrow."

Cassie looked crestfallen. "Go tonight, please. Me

and Mickey want to have a wedding. Gina said we could use her dress."

Hannah glanced at Gina. "You said that?"

"Yes, I did. But they've been forewarned that the groom will either be a stuffed animal or the baby brother, no boys from the neighborhood."

Cassie came to her feet and gave Hannah a hopeful look. "So can I stay, Mama? I'll be good and I'll help Mickey clean her room and I'll go to bed when I'm told."

Hannah couldn't in good conscience make a promise she might not keep. "We'll see. Right now you need to wash that purple eye shadow off your lids and go for something a little more subtle, like a nice beige. But before you do that, I want to take a picture."

While she fished her cell phone from her pocket, the girls struck a pose and put on their best grins. And as soon as she snapped the photo, the pair took off down the hall, sounds of sheer excitement echoing throughout the house.

She then noticed the blinking blue light indicating she'd received a text. And she couldn't be more surprised when she noted the message's sender. "Speak of the sexy devil."

Gina moved close to her side. "Devil as in the attorney?"

"Yes."

"What does it say?"

"'Dinner should be ready around seven. Italian. I also have a good bottle of wine. The only thing missing is you.'"

"Now I'm worried," Gina said.

Hannah pocketed the phone and stared at her friend. "You have something against Italian food?"

"I'm part Italian, silly. No, I'm worried because the devil didn't mention good sex."

She elbowed Gina in the side. "Would you please get off the sex thing? We have two impressionable, minor children in the house and they hear everything within a fifty-mile radius."

Gina pushed off the sofa and picked up the whimpering baby. "Come on, Hannah. Put on your big-girl panties and get with the program."

Something suddenly dawned on her. "Oh, my gosh, all I have are big-girl panties. Not a sexy pair in the drawer."

Her friend claimed the rocker across from the sofa and positioned the baby on her shoulder. "It's not even close to noon yet, so you have a few hours left to remedy that. Have you used the department-store gift card I gave you on your birthday?"

She was somewhat ashamed she'd held on to it for three months. "No, but before you get *your* big-girl panties in a wad, I've been too busy to shop."

"You better get busy if you want to be in Cheyenne by sundown," Gina said as she set the rocker in motion and rubbed her sleepy son's back.

A barrage of memories assaulted Hannah, recollections of a time when she'd rocked her baby girl, plagued with emotions that ran the gamut from bliss to utter sadness that her daughter's father would never know those precious moments. She secretly longed to have another child someday, and to be able to share that with a special someone. She suspected Logan Whittaker might not be the one to fulfill that dream.

"What's wrong now, Hannah?"

She looked at Gina through misty eyes. "Nothing really. Just remembering when Cassie was a baby, I guess. Time has a way of zipping by before you even realize it's gone."

"True, and time's a wastin' for you," Gina said. "Go shopping and buy those sexy panties along with a few nice outfits. Then go home and pack and get thee to Cheyenne."

If only it were that easy. "Do you really think this is the right thing to do?"

Gina sighed. "I think you'll never know unless you try, so just stop thinking and do it."

Her best friend was right. Nothing ventured, nothing gained, and all that jazz.

She might live to regret the decision, but darned if she wasn't actually going to do it.

Four

Never in a million years had Logan believed she'd actually do it. But there Hannah stood on his threshold, wearing a fitted, long-sleeved blue silk blouse covering tapered jeans, a small silver purse clutched in her hands. Talk about feeling underdressed in his faded navy T-shirt, tattered jeans and rough-out work boots. She'd parked her car beneath the portico and set two bags at her feet, which sported some deadly black heels, causing Logan to think questionable thoughts he shouldn't be thinking before she even made it into the house.

"You're here," he said, slight shock in his tone.

"I guess I should have called," she replied, clear concern in her voice.

"I told you to surprise me."

"Yes, but you looked absolutely stunned when you opened the door."

He grinned. "I thought you were the maid."

Fortunately she returned his smile. "I suppose we're going to have to work on that mistaken identity thing."

He personally would have to work on resisting the urge to kiss her at every turn. "We can do that after dinner."

"As long as I don't have to cook, it's a deal."

After grabbing Hannah's bags, Logan stepped aside and nodded toward the open door. "Come inside and make yourself at home."

The minute she entered the house, Hannah's gaze traveled upward toward the two-story foyer flanked by twin staircases with modern black banisters. "Wow. This is amazing."

He'd pretty much taken the view for granted and enjoyed seeing it through her eyes. "Yeah, it's impressive. But overall the place is more comfortable than elaborate."

She shot him a cynical look. "It's practically a mansion."

He started up the wood-covered stairs to the right. "I'll show you to your room before I give you the grand tour."

Hannah followed behind him to the second floor, where Logan stopped at the landing, allowing her to move in front of him for a purely selfish, and very male reason—to check out her butt. "Just go right and keeping walking until you reach the end of the hall."

She paused to peer inside the first of the three spare bedrooms. "Very nicely appointed. I really like the navy stripes mixed with yellows."

A color pallet he wouldn't have personally chosen, but if it worked for her, it worked for him. "The house was basically move-in ready. You can thank my decorator for the finishing touches. That's definitely not my thing."

"She's very good at what she does. I'm sure she has clients lined up for her services."

"Actually, she doesn't decorate for a living. She's a good friend of mine."

"A really good friend?"

When he heard the mild suspicion in Hannah's tone, he knew exactly what she was thinking. "Her name is Marlene and she's sixty years old. I'll introduce you in the near future." He decided to withhold the fact the woman was the late J. D. Lassiter's sister-in-law.

She passed the bathroom and peeked inside, then did the same with the next guest room, and pulled up short when she came to the closed door. "What's in here?"

A room he hadn't had the heart to touch, even if it did unearth bittersweet memories he'd just as soon forget. "It's a kid's bedroom that I haven't redone yet. I figured since I have three more guest rooms, I'm not in any hurry."

When she glanced back at him, Logan could tell she wasn't buying it. "Are you sure it's not your secret man-cave?"

"That's downstairs," he said, relieved she wasn't as suspicious as he'd assumed.

"Mind if I take a look?" she asked.

"Knock yourself out."

When Hannah opened the door and stepped inside, her expression said it all. The place was a little girl's fairy tale come to life, from the four princesses painted on the walls, to the pink cushioned seat built in beneath a ceiling-high window overlooking the courtyard at the front of the house.

"Cassie would absolutely love this," Hannah said as she looked around in awe. "That was one lucky little girl."

At least someone's little girl had been that lucky. "It's not exactly my taste, but then as a kid I preferred all things rodeo and baseball."

She turned and smiled. "Is that the décor you chose for your man-cave?"

His presumed "man-cave" would suit both genders. "You can see for yourself after we get you settled in, so keep going because we're almost there."

She turned and bowed. "My wish is your command, captain."

Grinning, he headed back into the hall and strode to the door he'd intentionally kept closed just so he could enjoy her reaction when he opened it. As expected, Hannah looked completely awed when he revealed the orange-tinted skies and the Rocky Mountain backdrop in clear view through the floor-to-ceiling windows.

"That is unbelievable," she said.

So was Logan's immediate physical reaction to the breathless quality of her voice. Keeping a firm grip on his control, he set her bags on the bench at the end of the king-size bed. "I have to agree with you there. It's better than the view from my bedroom, but you'll see that for yourself." When he noticed the trepidation in Hannah's eyes, he decided to backtrack for the second time in the past five minutes. "It's included on the tour, unless you want me to leave it off."

She shook her head. "No. Since we're both grown-ups, I can go into your bedroom without the fear of being grounded."

He wouldn't mind keeping her there for an indeterminate amount of time, a fact he'd keep to himself for now. "The bathroom's to your left."

She breezed through the bedroom, opened the double doors and then looked back with a smile. "Is this where you hold all your parties?"

He wouldn't mind holding a party there for the two of them. "Nope, but I probably could fit six people in the steam shower, and at least four in the jetted bathtub."

Hannah moved inside and ran her hand over one of the two granite-topped vanities. "I feel like I've died and gone to five-star-hotel heaven."

He thought he might die if he didn't get a little lip action real soon. "It's yours to enjoy for the duration."

She turned and leaned back against the vanity. "I could use a good soak in the tub."

And he'd gladly soak with her. "If you can wait until after dinner, that would be preferable. And speaking of that, it won't be too long before it's ready."

Hannah straightened and smiled. "Great, because I'm starving."

Man, so was he—for her undivided attention. "Then let's get going with the tour." Before he suggested they say to hell with dinner and take advantage of that tub. He definitely didn't want her to believe he intended to take advantage of her.

Logan showed Hannah to the upstairs den and then escorted her downstairs. He did a quick pass through the great room, pointed out his office and the game room, pausing as he arrived at the last stop before he led her to kitchen. "And this is my favorite place, the media room," he said as he opened the heavy double doors.

Her gaze traveled over the dark gray soundproof walls as she strolled down the black-carpeted, declining aisle. She paused to run her hand along the arm of one beige leather chair before facing him again. "Media room? This is more like an honest-to-goodness movie theater. All that's missing is a popcorn machine."

He nodded to his left. "In the corner behind that curtain, next to the soda fountain."

"Of course."

Hannah sounded almost disapproving, which sent Logan into defense mode. "Hey, the whole setup was here when I bought the house, including a huge collection of movies." Most of which he'd never watched because he didn't like watching alone. He planned to remedy that…and soon.

After folding her arms beneath her breasts, she slowly approached him. "I'd love to check out your collection."

"Not a problem, but right now I better check on dinner before I burn everything to a crisp and we have to call out for pizza."

She made a sweeping gesture toward the exit. "After you."

She followed quietly behind him as he led the way back through the great room and into the kitchen. As she'd done in the media room, Hannah took a visual trek through the area, her eyes wide with wonder. "State-of-the-art appliances, enough cabinets to store supplies for an army and a stainless island that I would sell my soul to have. Are you sure you don't have a robot hidden away somewhere to prepare your food?"

At least she'd said it with a smile, and that relieved him. He'd never been one to seek approval, but for some reason her opinion mattered. "No robot. Just me and sometimes the maid. I learned to cook after the divorce. It was either that or starve."

Hannah claimed the chrome-and-black bar stool across from the oven and folded her hands before her. "I hope it tastes as good as it smells."

He rounded the island, rested his elbows on the silver counter and angled his lower body away. "The recipe's never failed me before." He couldn't say the same for his self-control because he was having one hell of a fantasy involving her and that bar stool.

"What are we having?" she asked.

He personally was having a major desire to kiss her. "The mostaccioli I told you about."

"Fantastic. I've never had it before, but it's always good to try something new."

"And it's great to share something new with someone who's never experienced it before."

"I'm looking forward to a lot of new experiences while I'm here."

As their gazes remained connected, tension as apparent as the smell of the pasta hung in the air, until Hannah broke their visual contact by leaning around him. "According to your timer, we still have five minutes."

He straightened and glanced behind him before regarding her again. "True, and it needs to rest for another ten." Now what to talk about during those few minutes that would keep him from taking an inadvisable risk. "How did your daughter feel about you coming here?"

Hannah frowned. "She couldn't get me out of town fast enough. I can't compete with best friends and their baby brothers."

"I guess sometimes kids need a break from their parents."

She sighed softly. "I agree, but this is the longest break from each other we've ever had. I am glad to know she's in good hands, and that she's going to have a great time in my absence dressing up like a teenage harlot."

"Oh, yeah?"

Hannah pulled her cell phone from her pocket, hit an app and turned it around. "I took this photo this morning of my kiddo and her best friend, Michaela."

Logan started to laugh but the urge died when he homed in on the little girl standing next to Hannah's daughter. The resemblance might be slight, but the memories overwhelmed him. Recollections of his black-haired baby girl they'd appropriately named Grace.

He swallowed hard before handing Hannah the phone. "Gotta love their imaginations."

"Yes, but I don't like the fact she's trying to grow up too fast."

He'd give up everything he owned for the opportunity to watch his daughter grow up, but she'd been torn from his life after only four brief years. Now might be a good time to tell Hannah about her, but he wasn't ready yet. He wasn't sure he would ever be ready to make that revelation. "While we're waiting on dinner, do you want a glass of wine?"

"Sure," she said with a soft smile. "As long as you're also partaking tonight. I've decided it's best I not drink alone."

He'd learned that lesson all too well. "I'm not much of a wine drinker, but I do like a beer now and then."

"Whatever works for you."

Everything about Hannah Armstrong worked for him, and he'd just have to take out that thought and analyze it later. At the moment he needed to play the good host.

Logan crossed the room to a small bar where he'd set out an expensive bottle of red and poured a glass. Then he bent down and pulled out his favorite lager from the beverage refrigerator.

He returned to his place across from Hannah and slid the wine toward her. "Let me know if this meets your standards."

"I'm sure it will since I can only afford the cheap stuff," she said. "And before you mention that I can afford the best if I take the millions, don't waste your breath. I still haven't changed my mind."

"That's fine by me." And it was, to a point. "If you do refuse the inheritance, the funds will be merged into the Lassiter Foundation and given to charity."

She looked slightly amazed. "I didn't think J.D. would have a charitable bone in his body after the way he apparently treated my mother."

"And you," Logan said. "But he always has been somewhat of a philanthropist, and a good parent, which is why I'm surprised he would ignore his child."

"Perhaps he did have his reasons, and chances are I won't know. Maybe I don't want to know."

He didn't want to spoil the evening by being bogged

down by emotional chains from the past. "Let's concentrate on the present and worry about the rest later."

Hannah grinned and lifted her glass. "Here's to procrastination."

This time Logan did laugh as he touched his beer to her wine. "And to good food, new friends and more good food."

She took a sip of her wine and set the glass down. "Just don't feed me too well. If I put on an extra five pounds that means I'll have to lose fifteen instead of ten."

"You don't need to lose weight," he said, and he meant it. "You look great."

She lowered her gaze for a moment. "Thank you, but I really need to get back in shape so I can comfortably do those backflips."

That made him grin again. "I've got quite a few acres if you want to practice after dinner."

"Do you really think that's a good idea in the dark?"

No, but he could think of several things he'd like to do with her in the dark. Or the daylight. "You're right. I have another place to show you anyway."

She bent her elbow and supported her jaw with her palm. "Where do you plan to take me?"

Places she hadn't been before, but he didn't want to jump the gun, or get his hopes up...yet. "It's my second favorite place."

She narrowed her eyes. "You aren't referring to your bedroom since you left it off the tour, are you?"

He'd done that intentionally in an effort not to move too fast. "Not even close."

"Can you give me a hint?"

Without regard to the taking-it-slowly plan, he

reached over and brushed a strand of silky auburn hair from her cheek. "You surprised me tonight. Now it's time for me to surprise you."

Hannah had to admit she was a bit surprised when Logan suggested an after-dinner walk. She was even more shocked by his skill as a chef. Never before had she sampled such great food at the hands of a culinary hobbyist, who also happened to be a man.

She imagined his skills went far beyond the kitchen, particularly when it came to the bedroom. And although she'd been curious to see his sleeping quarters, she appreciated that he hadn't presented her with that possible temptation. Of course, she had no reason to believe he actually wanted to get her in his bed. She could hear Gina laughing at her naiveté the minute that thought vaulted into her brain.

According to Logan, the temperature had dropped quite a bit and now hovered around forty-five degrees, sending Hannah upstairs to change right after they cleaned the kitchen together. Hopefully the weather would begin to warm up in the next few days with the arrival of May. She rifled through her unpacked bag and withdrew a sweatshirt. After putting that on, she exchanged her heels for a pair of sneakers, did a quick makeup check, brushed her hair and then sprinted back down the stairs.

She found Logan waiting for her at the back door right off the mudroom adjacent to the kitchen, exactly where he'd told her to be. "I'm ready to walk off all that delicious food."

He inclined his head and studied her. "You really thought it was that good?"

Men. Always looking to have their egos stroked, among other things. She would actually be game for both…and obviously she was turning into a bad, bad girl. "I believe I said that at least five times during dinner, when I wasn't making the yummy noises."

His beautiful smile lit up his intriguing brown eyes. "Just making sure."

After Logan opened the door, Hannah stepped in front of him and exited the house. She was totally stunned, and extremely thrilled, when he rested his palm on the small of her back as he guided her toward a somewhat visible rock path illuminated by a three-quarter moon.

Unfortunately he dropped his hand as they began their walk toward a large expanse of land, but the Rocky Mountains silhouetted against the star-laden sky proved to be a great distraction. "It's really nice outside, even if it's a little cold."

"Feels good to me," he said.

She glanced at him briefly before turning her focus straight ahead to prevent tripping. "I can't believe you're not freezing since you're only wearing a light-weight jacket."

"The wind's not nearly as bad as it usually is around here. And I'm also pretty hot-blooded."

She had no doubt about that. He was hot, period. "What's that building in the distance?"

"A barn."

"Is that where you're taking me?"

"Nope."

She didn't quite understand why he seemed bent on being evasive. "Are you purposefully trying to keep me in suspense?"

"Yeah, but it'll be worth it."

A roll in the hay in the barn would be well worth it to her, and she'd best keep her questionable opinions to herself.

They continued to walk in silence until a smooth-wire fence stopped their forward progress. "This is my second favorite place," Logan said as he propped one boot on the bottom rail and rested his elbow on the top.

Hannah moved beside him and waited for her vision to adjust to the dark before taking in the panorama. The lush pasture traveled at an incline to what appeared to be a stream lined by a few trees. Not far away, she noticed two shadowy animals with their heads bent to graze on the grass. "Are those your horses?"

"Yeah. Harry and Lucy."

"Didn't they star in a fifties sitcom?"

Logan's laughter cut through the quiet. "I'm not sure about that, but they both came to me already named."

After she turned toward him and leaned against a post, his profile drew her attention. It was utterly perfect, from forehead to chin. "How long have you had them?"

"I bought Harry when I turned eighteen. He was a year-old gelding. I broke him and trained him to be a pretty good cutting horse. He's twenty now."

She had no idea what a cutting horse was, but she didn't want to show her ignorance. "What about Lucy?"

He went suddenly silent for a few seconds before speaking again. "I've had her about ten years, I guess. She's a retired pleasure horse and pretty kid-proof."

"That sounds about my speed."

He lowered his foot and faced her. "You've never ridden a horse?"

She internally cringed at the thought. "Twice. The first time I was sixteen and I went on a trail ride with friends. A controlled environment is a good place to start, or so they told me. They didn't, however, tell Flint, my ride. He decided to take off ahead of the pack and it took every ounce of my strength to get him to stop. After that, the trail master tied him to his horse to make sure he behaved."

"But you still got on a horse again?"

"On a beach in Mexico. I rode a really sweet mare and by the end of the ride, I'd trusted her enough to actually gallop." She closed her eyes and immersed herself in the memories. "The wind was blowing through my hair and the sun was on my face and I remember feeling the ocean spray on my feet. It was incredible."

"You're incredible."

She opened her eyes to find him staring at her. "Why?"

"Most people aren't brave enough to get back on a horse after a bad experience. I'm starting to wonder if anything scares you."

She was scared by the way she felt around him— ready to jump headfirst into possible heartache. "Believe me, I have fears like everyone else. I've just tried not to let them paralyze me."

Logan inched closer and streamed a fingertip along her jaw. "Would you be afraid if I kissed you again?"

She might die if he didn't. "Not really."

He bent and brushed a soft kiss across her cheek. "Would it scare you if I told you that you're all I've thought about for the past two days?"

"Would it scare you if I said I've been thinking about you, too?"

"I'm glad, because I can't get thoughts of us, being really close, off my mind." When he laced their fingers together, the implications weren't lost on Hannah.

"It's been a long time, Logan. I don't take intimacy lightly."

"I respect that," he said, not sounding the least bit disappointed. "That's why I only want to kiss you. Tonight."

After he said it, he did it, and he did it very well. The first time she'd kissed him, she'd fumbled through the motions. The first time he'd kissed her, he'd been quick about it. But not now.

He explored her mouth with care, with the gentle stroke of his tongue, allowing her to capture all the sensations. She responded with a soft moan and a certain need to be closer to him. On that thought, she wrapped her hands around his waist while he wound one hand through her hair and planted the other on her back.

When Logan tugged her flush against him, the cold all but disappeared, replaced by a searing heat that shot the length of Hannah's body and came to rest in unseen places, leaving dampness in its wake.

Too long since she'd been kissed this way, felt this way. Too long since she'd experienced a desire so strong that if Logan laid her down on the hard ground beneath their feet and offered to remove her clothes, she'd let him.

Clearly Logan had other ideas, she realized, when he broke the kiss and tipped his forehead against hers. "I need you so damn bad I hurt."

She'd noticed that need when she'd been pelvis-to-pelvis with him. "Chemistry definitely can commandeer your body."

He pulled back and studied her eyes. "But I don't want to screw this up, Hannah, so we're going to take this slowly. Get to know each other better. But sweetheart, before you leave, I plan to make love to you in ways you won't forget."

Hannah trembled at the thought. "You're mighty confident, Mr. Whittaker."

"I just know what I want when I want it, and I want you." He ran the tip of his tongue over the shell of her ear and whispered, "I think you want me just as badly. So let's go before I change my mind and take you down on the ground and get you naked."

Her body reacted with another surge of heat and dampness over Logan's declaration. Yet they walked back to the house, hand in hand, like innocent young lovers who'd just discovered each other, not mature adults who were approaching the point of no return.

Hannah knew better than to cross that line too soon. She knew better than to lead with her heart and not her head. Yet when Logan said goodbye to her at the bedroom door, she almost tossed wisdom out the window for a night of wild abandon. Instead, she let him go and sought out the place where she would spend the night alone longing for things she shouldn't. Wanting, needing, Logan's words echoing through her cluttered mind…

But sweetheart, before you leave, I plan to make love to you in ways you won't forget…

Deep down she had no doubt he was a man of his word. But if she took that leap into lovemaking, would her heart suffer another devastating blow?

Five

"What do you mean you didn't do it?"

That was the last thing Hannah wanted to hear first thing in the morning, especially from her best friend.

After turning the cell on speaker and setting it on the bed beside her, she slid a sneaker onto her foot and began lacing it. "He happens to be a gentleman, Gina. And I didn't call to talk about my sex life. I called to talk to my daughter."

"You don't have a sex life, and you can't talk to Cassie because she's not here right now."

She tightened the shoestrings just a little too tight. "Where is she?"

"Out with bikers she met bar-hopping last night."

Infuriating woman. "I'm serious, Regina Gertrude Romero."

"You know how I hate it when you use my middle name."

"Yes, I do," she said as she pulled on the remaining shoe. "Now tell me my daughter's actual whereabouts before I tell everyone in your book club that you want to be a pole dancer when you finally grow up."

Gina let out an exaggerated sigh. "She's with Frank at his sister's house. Since it's going to be close to eighty degrees today, and we don't know how long this heat wave is going to last, the kids are going to swim."

Hannah was poised to hit the panic button. "Are you sure it's warm enough there because it's not nearly that warm here."

"I checked the weather, Hannah. And don't forget, you're almost a hundred miles away."

She hadn't forgotten that at all, and now the distance between her and her child really worried her. "I hope the adults pay close attention because Cassie—"

"Can swim better than you and me," Gina said. "Stop being such a worrywart."

Her patience was starting to unravel. "Did you pack sunscreen? You know how easily she burns."

"Yes, I did, and I put the fire department on alert, just in case."

One more acerbic comment and she might very well come completely unglued. "Real funny, Regina. And why are you home?"

"Trey kept me up a good part of the night, so Frank let me sleep in while the baby is sleeping. I'll be heading out in an hour or so. By the way, where is your attorney now?"

He wasn't *her* attorney, but Hannah saw no reason to debate that point. "I'm not sure. I just got out of the shower and I haven't left the bedroom yet."

"I could see where you'd still be in the bedroom if

he was in there with you, but it's almost ten o'clock. Don't you think he might be wondering if you've flown the coop, leaving the rooster all alone?"

Hannah had thought about that, but so far she hadn't heard a thing coming from downstairs. "Maybe he's sleeping in, too. But I won't know until I get off the phone."

"Hint taken. Call me this evening and I'll put your daughter on the phone, unless, of course, you're engaged in some serious cross-examination."

"I'm hanging up now, Gina." As soon as she ended the call, Hannah hopped to her feet, ready to face the day—and Logan.

After a quick makeup application and hair brushing, she sprinted down the stairs, tugging at her plain light blue T-shirt and wishing she'd worn a better pair of jeans. But casual seemed to suit Logan. Very well.

She wound her way through the cowboy palace, following the scent of coffee in hopes of locating the master of the manor. When she arrived in the kitchen, there he was in all his glory, sitting with his back to her at the island. He wore a navy plaid flannel shirt and a cowboy hat, which almost sent Hannah completely into a female frenzy over her Wild West fantasy coming to life.

She stood in the kitchen opening just long enough to take a good look at his broad back before she slid onto the stool across from him. "Good morning."

He lifted his gaze from his coffee cup and smiled, but only halfway. "Mornin', ma'am. How did you sleep?"

Like a woman who couldn't get his kisses off her

blasted mind. "Pretty darn well, thank you. That mattress is as soft as a cloud."

"I'm glad you found the accommodations satisfactory." He nodded at the counter behind her. "There's some coffee left if you want me to get you a cup."

"I'll get some in a minute," she said when she noticed the keys resting near his right hand. "Have you been out already this morning?"

"Not yet, but unfortunately I'm going to have to get a move on. I got a call from Chance Lassiter. He's Marlene's son and the ranch manager at the Big Blue. He needs some extra help herding a few calves that got out of a break in the fence last night."

It figured her plans would be foiled by a Lassiter. So much for spending a relaxing Sunday getting to know him better. "How long will that take?"

"Hard to say, but it could be quite a while since we'll need to cover a lot of land. And the ranch is about thirty minutes north of here. Feel free to turn on the TV while I'm gone, or use the computer if you want to do some research on the Lassiters. If you need supplies, they're in the desk drawer."

She wondered why he would invite her—a virtual stranger—into his private domain. "You're absolutely sure you don't mind me hanging out in your office?"

He sent her a sexy-as-sin grin. "I don't have anything to hide. All my professional files are password protected, but if you have a hankerin' to hack into those, knock yourself out. The legal jargon on mergers and acquisitions is pretty damn riveting. Just be forewarned you're going to need a nap afterward."

She wouldn't mind taking a nap with him. "Do you want me to whip something up for dinner?"

"Don't worry about me. As far as you're concerned, there's quite a bit of food in the refrigerator, so help yourself."

Hannah admittedly was a bit disappointed he hadn't asked her to join him on the day trip. "Thanks."

"I really hate having to leave you, but—"

"I'm a big girl, Logan. I can entertain myself until you return."

He reached over the counter and ran a fingertip along her jaw. "When I get back, I have some entertainment in mind for you."

She shivered like a schoolgirl at the thought. "And what will that entail?"

After he stood, Logan rounded the island, came up behind her and brought his mouth to her ear. "You'll just have to wait and see, but it will be worth the wait."

After Hannah shifted toward him, Logan gave her a steamy kiss that made her want to initiate his kitchen counter. Or the floor. But he pulled away before she could act on impulse.

He snatched up his keys and winked. "I'll let you know when I'm heading home."

"I'll be here." And she couldn't think of any place she would rather be at the moment, aside from home with her daughter. Or in bed with him.

Naughty, naughty, Hannah.

After Logan left out the back door, she hurried to the great room to peer out the picture window facing the front drive. She waited until he guided the massive black dual-wheel truck and silver horse trailer onto the main road before she returned to the kitchen for coffee. She poured a cup and doctored it with lots of sugar and cream, then ate the apple set out in a fruit bowl.

Now what? TV watching seemed about as appealing as contemplating the cosmos. She did bring a book, but she wasn't in the mood to read. Doing a little research on Logan's computer called to her curiosity. After finishing off the coffee, she went in search of his office and retraced her steps from when Logan showed her around. Following a few wrong turns, she finally located the room beyond the formal dining room.

The French doors were closed, but not locked, allowing Hannah easy entry into the attorney's inner sanctum. A state-of-the-art PC sat in the center of a modern black desk that looked remarkably neat. Two walls of matching bookshelves housed several law manuals, as well as quite a few true-crime novels.

She dropped into the rolling black leather chair and scooted close to the computer, ready to start looking for more info on the Lassiters. Yet something else immediately drew her attention.

In Hannah's opinion, a man's desk drawer was equivalent to a medicine cabinet—worthy of investigation. But did she dare poke around? That would undeniably be considered an invasion of privacy. Sort of. Hadn't he said to help herself to any supplies? Of course, she didn't need any paper or pens yet, but she did have a strong need to satisfy her nosiness.

With that in mind, Hannah slid the drawer open slowly, and like the desk, the thing was immaculate. She took a quick inventory after she didn't notice anything out of the ordinary on first glance. A few pens in a plastic divider, along with some binder clips. A box of staples. A stack of stationery stamped with his name, along with coordinating envelopes.

Not quite satisfied, Hannah pulled the drawer open

as far as she could, and glimpsed the corner of something shiny. She lifted the brown address book to find a small silver frame etched with teddy bears and balloons, the bottom stamped with a date—February 15, twelve years ago. She withdrew the photo of a pretty newborn with a dark cap of hair, a round face, precious puckered lips and what looked to be a tiny dimple imprinted on its right cheek. Unfortunately, she couldn't quite determine the gender due to the neutral yellow gown, but she would guess this baby happened to be a little girl. The question was, *whose* little girl?

Logan had been adamant he had no children, leaving Hannah to assume the infant could be a sibling's child, if he had any siblings. She could clear up the mystery when he came home, but since the frame had been tucked away out of sight, she would have to admit she'd been snooping.

Right now she had another mystery that needed her focus, namely trying to find any clues indicating John Douglas Lassiter was her mother's sperm donor.

With that in mind, Hannah booted the computer and brought up her favorite search engine. She decided to dig a little deeper this time, expand her inquiries, and learn as much about the Lassiter family as possible, beginning with where it had all begun. She read articles about the self-made billionaire and his various ventures, from newspapers to cattle to his media corporation in California. He'd married a woman named Ellie, adopted her two nephews and lived through the loss of his wife, who sadly died at forty-two just days after giving birth to a daughter.

She took a few moments to study a recent publicity photo of that daughter, Angelica Lassiter, who could possibly be her sister. The sophisticated-looking woman was tall and slimly built, with dark hair and eyes—nothing that physically indicated Hannah might be kin to the reported "brains" behind Lassiter Media. Apparently Angelica had broken off her engagement to Evan McCain, interim chairman and CEO of the company, after a reported dispute over the terms in her father's will. High drama indeed.

Hannah surfed a little longer, trying to establish some connection between J.D. and her mother, yet she found nothing whatsoever to prove that theory.

Stiff-necked and bleary-eyed, Hannah noticed the time and realized a good part of the day had already passed her by. And as far as she knew, Logan hadn't returned home yet. She sat back in the chair and closed her eyes, remembering his lips fused with hers, his body pressed flush against her body, how badly she had wanted him last night. How badly she wanted him still, though she shouldn't…

The phone shrilled, startling Hannah so badly, she nearly vaulted from the rolling chair as she fumbled the cell from her pocket. Disappointment washed over her when Gina's name—not Logan's—displayed on the screen. "No, we haven't done it yet."

"Done what, Mama?"

Great. This was not the way she wanted to introduce her child to human sexuality. "Hi, sweetie. I miss you. Do you miss me?"

"Uh-huh, a little."

That stung Hannah like a hornet. "Are you back at Gina's?"

"Nope. We're still at Aunt Linda's house and we're swimming a lot."

Funny how Cassie had adopted the Romero family's relatives. But then she had very few relatives aside from Danny's parents. For the most part, they didn't count. "Are you sunburned?"

"A little on my nose. I'm gonna get more freckles, right?"

She was somewhat surprised that her daughter sounded almost happy about it. "If you continue to stay in the sun, yes, you probably will."

"Or if I swallow a nickel and break out in pennies."

"Where did you hear that, Cassie?"

"Frank told me. I like Frank. I wish he was my daddy. I mean, I love my daddy in heaven, but I want a real one. Mickey said she'd share him."

Hannah's heart took a little dip in her chest when she recalled how difficult it had been to grow up without a father. At least Cassie knew who her dad was, even if she'd never known him. She also had many pictures of Danny available to look at any time she desired. "Well, honey, maybe someday that might happen."

"Are you gonna marry your prince?"

Cassie sounded so hopeful Hannah hated to burst her fairy-tale bubble. "If you mean Mr. Whittaker, he's a lawyer, not a prince, and he's only my friend."

"But he's really cute and he doesn't have a kid. Everyone should have a kid."

From the mouth of her matchmaking babe.

Hannah heard a background voice calling for Cassie to come on, followed by her daughter saying, "Gotta go, Mama. We're eating pizza!"

"Okay, sweetie, tell Gina that—"

When she heard a click, Hannah checked to see if the call had ended, which it had. The conversation had been too brief for her liking, and too telling, yet she understood Cassie's excitement over being a part of a complete family.

At some point in time, perhaps she could provide that family for her daughter, but she didn't believe it would happen in the foreseeable future. And definitely not with Prince Logan. Though she didn't know the details of his divorce, she sensed he wasn't willing to travel that road again. Regardless, she would enjoy their time together and let whatever happened, happen. Now that she knew Cassie was faring well without her, she wasn't in a rush to head home.

"What is the rush to leave, Logan Whittaker?"

If he answered the question, it would require explaining his houseguest to Marlene Lassiter. And although she was as good as gold, she had a penchant for trying to direct his private life. "I'm just ready to take a shower and prepare for work tomorrow." And get home to a woman who'd weighed on his mind all day long.

She patted her short brown hair before pulling out a chair for him at the dining table in the corner of the kitchen area. "You've got time to eat. I made my famous meat loaf and cornbread."

Logan hadn't realized he was hungry until she'd said the magic words. Nothing like good old country cooking. He hadn't checked in with Hannah yet, so she wasn't expecting him. That didn't discount the fact he was still in a hurry to get home to her. "Do you mind fixing me a plate to go?"

That earned him Marlene's frown as she hovered above him. "Do you have a meeting of some sort?"

"Not exactly."

"Could—wonder of wonders—you have a date?"

If he didn't throw her a bone, she'd keep hounding him. "I have a friend staying with me and I'd like to get in a visit before I go to bed." Among other things.

Marlene smoothed a hand down her full-length apron. "Well then, I'll just make up two plates since I wouldn't want *him* to go hungry."

Damn. He might as well correct the gender issue. "I'm sure *she'll* appreciate it."

Marlene pointed a finger at him. "Aha! I suspected you're harboring a woman."

That sounded like he was holding Hannah against her will. He turned the chair around backward and straddled it. "Before you start getting any wrong notions, she's just a friend."

Marlene walked into the nearby pantry, returned with two paper plates and began dishing out food from the stove. "Are you sure about that friend designation? One of the hands said you seemed distracted, and nothing distracts a man more than a woman."

Double damn. "Just because I temporarily lost one of the heifers that left the herd doesn't mean I was distracted. It happens."

She shot him a backward glance. "It doesn't happen to you. But I'm glad you're finally getting back into the dating scene."

He could set her straight, or let her think what she would. He chose the first option. "Look, I'm handling a legal matter for her. That's why she's here."

After covering the plates with foil, Marlene turned and leaned back against the counter. "Is there potential for it being more than a client-attorney relationship?"

"It might, but I'm not in the market for anything permanent at this point in time." If ever.

"Does she know this, or are you leading her on?"

She had an uncanny knack for seeing right through him. "I'm not going to do anything to hurt her, if that's what's worrying you. Besides, she doesn't strike me as the kind of woman who's looking to nab a husband. Not only is she widowed, she also has a five-year-old daughter to consider."

Marlene frowned. "Have you told her about Grace?"

He should've seen that coming. "You know I don't talk about that with anyone but you, and that's only because you prodded me about my past." After he'd had a few too many during a party she'd hosted that happened to have fallen on Grace's birthday. He'd spent the night on her couch and woken the next morning with a hangover and more than a handful of regrets over baring his soul.

"Maybe you should talk to someone else about her, Logan," she said. "Keeping all that guilt and grief bottled up isn't doing you any good. You can't move forward if you stay stuck in the past."

"I'm not stuck." He tempered his tone, which sounded way too defensive. "I like to keep my private life completely private."

"And if you keep that attitude, you're never going to be happy." She took the chair next to his. "Honey, you're a good man. You have a whole lot to offer the right woman. You can't let yourself get bogged down in mistakes you think you might have made. One day you're going to have to forgive yourself, go on with your life and take a chance on love again."

He *had* made mistakes. Unforgivable mistakes.

"Isn't that the pot-and-kettle thing, Marlene? You never remarried after Charles died."

Marlene turned her wedding band round and round her finger. "No, I didn't. But that doesn't mean I cut myself off from love."

Exactly what he'd assumed, along with everyone else in town. "You mean you and J.D."

"I didn't say that."

She didn't have to. Logan saw the truth in her hazel eyes. He'd also seen something else in her at J.D.'s funeral, that soul-binding sorrow that he'd known all too well. "Come on, Marlene. You lived here with J.D. all those years after you both lost your spouses. No one would fault the two of you for being close."

"He was totally devoted to the kids and Ellie's memory." She sighed. "His wife meant everything to him and he never really got over her."

Which meant Marlene's love could have been one-sided. "Are you going to deny he cared for you, too?"

She shook her head. "No, I'm not, because he did care. But I couldn't compete with his cherished ghost. Regardless, we had some very good times."

That led Logan to believe the pair had been lovers, not that he'd ever request verification. "I tell you what, when you decide to have a serious relationship again, then I'll consider it, too." He figured he was pretty safe with that pact.

Marlene smiled sagely. "You never know what the future holds."

After checking the clock on the wall, Logan came to his feet. "I better get back to the house, otherwise Hannah might not speak to me again."

"Hannah?" she asked, more concern than curiosity in her voice.

"Yeah. Hannah Armstrong. Why?"

She attempted another smile but it fell flat. "Nothing. I've always thought it's a lovely name for a girl."

Logan wasn't buying that explanation, but he didn't have the energy to question her further tonight. He'd set aside some time later and have a long talk with her. Marlene Lassiter's relationship with her brother-in-law could be the key to solving the mystery of Hannah's past.

Yeah, he'd wait a little while before he sought more information from Marlene. If she did hold the answers, then Hannah would no longer have any reason to stay. And he damn sure wasn't ready for her to leave.

She wasn't quite ready to leave the heavenly bath, but when Hannah heard sounds coming from downstairs, she realized the dashing attorney was finally home.

After extracting herself from the jetted tub, she hurriedly dried off and prepared to get ready to greet him. And since she'd had headphones stuck on her ears until a few minutes before, and she hadn't checked her cell for messages in the past hour, she had no idea when Logan had returned.

She quickly dressed in a white tank with built-in bra and black jeans, then had a crisis of confidence and covered the top with a coral-colored, button-down blouse. She brushed her teeth, applied subtle makeup and opted to leave her hair in the loose twist atop her head. Danny had often told her she looked sexy with her hair up…and she really shouldn't be thinking about him while in the home of another man. An undeniably sexy man who'd commandeered her common sense from the moment she'd met him. And that lack of common sense had her slipping the first three buttons on the blouse to reveal the lace-edged tank beneath. An obvious indication of a woman bent on seduction.

Bracing her palms on the vanity, Hannah leaned forward and studied the face in the mirror. The same face that looked back at her every morning. Yep, she looked the same, but she felt very different. Her nerves sang like a canary and she felt as if her skin might take a vacation without her.

What was she thinking? It took a good three months for her and Danny to consummate their relationship. She'd only known Logan for three days. Yet she was older, and wiser, and lonely. She wanted to be in the arms of a man she was beginning to trust. Why she trusted him, she couldn't say. Intuition? Or maybe she was simply so foggy from lust that she wasn't thinking straight at all. That didn't keep her from sliding her feet into a pair of silver sandals and dabbing on perfume when she thought she heard him calling her name.

After rushing out of the bathroom and jogging through the bedroom, Hannah stopped in the hall to catch her breath. Seeming too enthusiastic might lead to misunderstanding. She might be happy to see him. She might be game for a little more serious necking. But she didn't know if she had the courage to go any farther than that.

She took her sweet time walking down the stairs and basically strolled to the great room. When she didn't find Logan there, she entered the kitchen to find it deserted as well. She did discover a pair of boots in the mudroom and his keys hanging on the peg, and detected the sound of the dryer in the adjacent utility room that was about as large as her den back in Boulder. At least she hadn't imagined he'd returned, but maybe she *had* imagined he'd called her.

Determined to locate the missing lawyer, she explored all the rooms he'd shown her, to no avail. That left her with only one uncharted location—his bedroom. She didn't dare go there. If he needed to speak with her, he could come and get her.

Two hours had passed since she'd eaten the ham sandwich, so she retrieved a bottle of water from the fridge and then perused the pantry for some sort of snack. She targeted the bananas hanging on the bronze holder and snapped off the best of the bunch.

Hannah had barely made herself at home on the bar stool when she heard heavy footfalls heading in her direction. The thought of seeing Logan gave her a serious case of goose bumps. When he walked into the kitchen, dressed in only a low-slung navy towel, she thought she'd been thrust into some nighttime soap opera starring a half-naked Hollywood hunk. He had a twelve-pack's worth of ridges defining his torso, a slight shading of hair between his pecs and another thin strip pointing downward to ground zero. Broad shoulders, toned biceps. Oh, boy. Oh, man.

While she sat there like a mime, appropriately clutching a phallic piece of fruit, Logan flashed her his dimpled grin. "You're here."

"You're wearing a towel." Brilliant, Hannah.

He pointed behind her. "I've got clothes in the dryer. I thought maybe you'd gone to bed already."

She noticed what looked to be a red tattoo on his upper right arm, but she couldn't see the details unless she asked him to turn toward her. Right now speaking at all was an effort, and the frontal view couldn't be beat. "It's not even six o'clock. I never go to bed that early."

"Maybe that theory was a stretch, but you didn't answer when I called you. And you didn't respond to my text."

She was surely responding to him now. All over. "I was taking a bath. The jets in the tub were going and I was listening to my MP3 player."

He cocked a hip against a cabinet and crossed his arms over his extremely manly chest. "Did you enjoy the bath?"

Not as much as she was enjoying the view right now. "Yes. Very relaxing. You should try it."

"I've got a big tub in my bathroom, but I'm not a bath kind of guy."

Maybe not, but he was one gorgeous guy. "Most men aren't into taking baths."

"True," he said. "Showers have always suited me better. A lot less effort. Easy in, easy out."

That conjured up images Hannah shouldn't be having. "I prefer showers, too, but I like a good bath now and then."

When he pushed away from the counter, she held her breath. She released it when he started toward the laundry room. "My clothes are probably dry now, so I better get dressed."

Please don't, she wanted to say, but stopped the comment threatening to burst out of her mouth. "Good idea."

The dryer door opened, followed by Logan calling, "If you're hungry, there's a plate of food in the refrigerator Marlene sent with me."

Hannah unpeeled the banana she still had in a death grip. "Thanks, but I've already eaten." She took a large bite of the fruit. Probably too large.

"Did you do any online research today?" he said over the sound of shuffling clothes.

"Yes, I did," she replied, her words muffled due to banana mouth.

"Find anything interesting?"

She swallowed this time before speaking. "Not much other than business articles." And a photo in his drawer that had piqued her interest.

While Hannah finished the fruit fest, Logan returned a few minutes later, fully dressed in beige T-shirt and old jeans. "I have an idea on how we might get some information on J.D.," he said.

She slid off the stool, opened the walk-in pantry and tossed the peel into the trash before facing him again. "What would that be?"

He leaned over the island using his elbows for support. "I'll let you know after I investigate further. It could end up being a dead end."

The man was nothing if not covert in his dealings. Must be the attorney thing—confidentiality at all costs. "Fine. Just let me know if you turn something up."

"I will." He straightened and smiled. "Are you in the mood for a little entertainment?"

She'd already been quite entertained by his recent show of bare flesh. "Sure. What do you suggest we do?"

"Watch a movie in the media room."

Not exactly what she had in mind, but what she'd been envisioning wouldn't be wise. "I'm all for a movie. Lead the way."

Six

Logan had chosen the lone theater chair built for two, along with a shoot-'em-up suspense film. But he hadn't bargained for the racy sex scene that came during the movie's first fifteen minutes.

He glanced to his right at Hannah, who had a piece of popcorn poised halfway to her mouth, her eyes wide as wagon wheels. "Wow. What is this rated?"

"R, but I thought that was due to the violence factor."

She popped a kernel into her mouth and swallowed. "I can't believe he didn't take off the shoulder holster when he dropped his pants. What if the gun goes off?"

"It does give a whole new meaning to 'cocked and ready.'" And he might have gone a bit too far with the crudeness.

Surprisingly, she released a soft, sultry laugh. "Ha, ha. It's hard for me to imagine a man taking a woman in an alley in broad daylight, gun or no gun."

That didn't exactly surprise him. "Anything's possible when you want someone bad enough." Exactly how he felt at the moment.

She tipped the red-striped box toward him. "Want some of this?"

His current appetite didn't include popcorn. "No thanks."

As the on-screen bumping and grinding continued, Logan draped his arm over the back of the seat, his hand resting on Hannah's shoulder. When he rubbed slow circles on her upper arm, she shifted closer to his side and laid her palm on his thigh. If she knew what was happening a little north of her hand, she might think twice about leaving it there. And if the damn movie didn't return to the run-and-gun scenes real soon, no telling what he might do.

No telling what *Hannah* might do was his immediate thought when she briefly nuzzled his neck, then brushed a kiss across his cheek. His second thought… the cheek kiss wasn't enough.

Logan tipped Hannah's face toward him and brought her mouth to his, intending only to kiss her once before going back to the film that fortunately now focused on the suspense plot. But the lengthy sex scene had obviously ignited the sparks between them, and from that point forward, everything began to move at an accelerated pace.

They made out like two teenagers on a curfew to the sounds of gunfire and cursing. He couldn't seem to get close enough to Hannah and that prompted him to pull her up onto his lap. He wound his hands through her hair and continued to kiss her like there was no tomorrow.

With Hannah's legs straddling his thighs, the contact was way too intimate for Logan to ignore. Every time she moved, he grew as hard as a hammer. To make matters worse, she broke the kiss, rose up and pulled away the band securing her lopsided ponytail. Obviously she was testing his sanity when she unbuttoned her blouse, slipped it off and tossed it aside, leaving her dressed in a thin tank top that left little to the imagination.

Seeing her sitting there with her tousled auburn hair falling to her shoulders, her lips slightly swollen and her green eyes centered on his, Logan's strength went the way of the popcorn that had somehow ended up on the floor. And just when he'd thought she was done with the surprises, she slid the straps off her shoulders and lowered the top.

He'd dimmed the lights before he'd cued the movie, but he could still make out the details. Incredible details. Unbelievable, in fact. Too tempting to not touch. That's exactly what he did—touched both her breasts lightly while watching her reaction. When Hannah tipped her head back and exhaled a shaky breath, Logan personally found it hard to breathe at all, and even harder not to take it further.

Pressing his left palm against her back, he nudged her forward and replaced his right hand with his mouth. Logan circled his tongue around one pale pink nipple, drawing out Hannah's soft groan. When he paid equal attention to her other breast, she shifted restlessly against his fly. If she didn't stop soon, it would be all over but the moaning. He damn sure didn't want to stop completely. He had a perfectly good bed at their disposal…and a perfectly good reason to halt the insanity before he couldn't. She deserved better than a quick roll in a chair, and he had no condoms available.

On that thought, he returned Hannah to the seat beside him and leaned back to stare at the soundproof ceiling while his respiration returned to normal.

"What was that?" Hannah asked, her voice somewhat hoarse.

Logan straightened to find her perched on the edge of the seat. Fortunately she'd pulled her top back into place, otherwise he wouldn't be able to concentrate. "That was uncontrollable lust."

"And, might I add, two adults acting like oversexed sixteen-year-olds," she said. "All we need now is to climb into the backseat of your car and have at it."

He didn't need to entertain that notion, but damned if he wasn't. "Hey, it happens."

"Not to me," she said. "I have never, ever been that bold."

He liked her boldness. A lot. "Not even with your husband?"

"Not really. We were both young when we met, and not very adventurous."

Interesting. "What about the men before him?"

Her gazed faltered for a moment. "Danny was my first. There wasn't anyone before him and there hasn't been anyone since."

Man, he hadn't predicted that. She kissed like someone who'd been around the block. Apparently she was a natural, even if she was somewhat of a novice. "Had I known that, I would've stopped sooner."

She frowned. "Why?"

"Because I don't want to do anything you don't want to do."

This time she released a cynical laugh. "I would think it's fairly obvious I wanted to do what I did, or I wouldn't have done it."

"Neither of us was thinking clearly." But he sure was now.

"Probably not, but since we're both consenting adults, I certainly don't consider our behavior shameful by any stretch of the imagination."

"I'm not sure I'm ready for this." He'd heard those words before, but never coming out of his own mouth.

Hannah looked perplexed. "Excuse me?"

He leaned forward, draped his elbows on his parted knees and focused on the popcorn-riddled carpet. "I'm not sure this is the right thing for either of us. More important, I don't want to hurt you, Hannah."

She touched his shoulder, garnering his attention. "I'm a big girl, Logan. I don't have any wild expectations of happily-ever-after. I want to feel desired by a man I can trust to treat me well. I know that man is you."

Yet she didn't know what he'd been concealing from her. She didn't know the demons still chasing after him. And she had no idea that his feelings for her were going beyond animal attraction.

He needed time to think. He needed to get away from her in order to keep his libido from prevailing over logic. Being the second man in her life would be a big burden to bear. He'd gained skill as a lover through experience, but he sucked when it came to the possible emotional fallout. If they continued on this course, they would only grow closer, and she might begin to have expectations he couldn't meet, regardless of what she'd said about not having any.

For that reason, he grabbed the remote from the adjacent chair, turned off the movie and stood. "I have an early day tomorrow and I'm pretty tired. We'll continue this discussion later."

Hannah stood and propped both hands on her hip. "That's it? You're going to run out on me without explaining why you've suddenly gone from hot to cold?"

He couldn't explain unless he made a few revelations that he wasn't prepared to make at this point. "I have some thinking to do, Hannah, and I can't do it with you in the same room."

"Suit yourself," she said as she moved past him and headed toward the exit.

He couldn't let her leave without telling her one important fact. "Hannah."

She turned at the door, anger glimmering in her eyes. "What?"

"I just don't want you to have any regrets."

"I don't," she said. "But I'm beginning to think you do."

Logan only regretted he might not be the man she needed. The man she deserved. And he had to take that out and examine it later before he made one huge error in judgment.

For the past two days, Hannah had barely seen Logan. He'd left for work before she'd awakened, and returned well after she'd retired to her room. She'd whiled away the lonely hours researching her possible family until she was certain her eyes might be permanently crossed. Her only human contact had come in the form of Logan's fiftysomething housekeeper,

Molly, who'd been extremely accommodating, right down to preparing meals in advance.

Of course, on several occasions she had spoken to Cassie, who had reinforced that she was having the time of her life with her best friend. Out of sight, out of mind, Hannah realized, at least when it came to her daughter and the attorney. And that hurt.

But after spending the morning in the public library perusing archived newspapers, Hannah had the perfect excuse to seek out Logan. She'd intentionally dressed in her professional best—a white sleeveless silk blouse, charcoal-colored skirt and black three-inch heeled sandals that Gina had fondly termed "do-me shoes." Hopefully she wasn't wasting those on a possible lost cause named Logan.

She didn't bother to call ahead before she arrived at the Drake, Alcott and Whittaker law firm located not far from the library. After playing tug-of-war with the strong Wyoming wind for control of the heavy wood door, she simply marched up to the very young, very pretty brunette receptionist and presented her best smile. "I need to see Mr. Whittaker please."

The young woman eyed Hannah suspiciously. "Do you have an appointment?"

She finger-combed her gale-blown hair back into place as best she could without a brush. "No, I don't. But I'm sure if you'll give him my name, he'll see me." If luck prevailed.

"What *is* your name?" the receptionist asked, sounding as if she believed Hannah might be some crazed stalker.

"It's Ms. Armstrong. Hannah Armstrong."

"Just a moment please." She picked up the phone and

pressed a button. "Mr. Whittaker, there's a Ms. Armstrong here and she… Of course. I'll send her right in." She replaced the phone and finally put on a pleasant demeanor. "His office is down the hall to your right, the second door on the left."

"Thank you."

Hannah traveled down the corridor with a spring in her step, feeling somewhat vindicated, until she realized she probably looked a whole lot disheveled. She paused long enough to open her bag for the appropriate tools, then brushed her hair and applied some lip gloss before continuing on to Logan's office. A brass plate etched with his name hung on the closed door, but the raised blinds covering the glass windows lining the hallway gave her a prime view of Logan, who happened to be on the phone.

She wasn't sure whether to wait until he hung up, or barge in. She opted to wait, until Logan caught her glance and gestured at her to come in.

Hannah stepped into the office, closed the door behind her and chose the chair across from the large mahogany desk. In an attempt not to appear to be eavesdropping, she surveyed the office while Logan continued his conversation. She had three immediate impressions—massive, masculine and minimalist. Neutral colors with dark blue accents, including the sofa and matching visitors' chairs. Blue-and-white-tiled fireplace with a barren mantel. A few modern Western paintings. Overall, a nice place to visit, but she wouldn't care to work there. The whole area could use some warming up.

Hannah couldn't say the same for herself. Seeing the sexy attorney dressed in coat and tie, his dark hair combed to perfection, his large hand gripping the phone, she had grown quite warm.

He seemed to be listening more than speaking until he finally said, "I understand, Mom, and I promise to do better with the calls. Tell Dad to stop giving you grief, and I'll talk to you next week. I love you, too." He then hung up and sent her a somewhat sheepish grin. "Sorry about that."

"I think it's nice you're close to your mother." The kind of relationship she'd wanted with hers, but never really had. "Are you an only child?"

"Actually, no," he said. "I have an older sister. She and her husband are both geologists living in Alaska with their five kids."

That could explain the picture in his desk drawer. "Wow. Five kids, huh?"

He grabbed a pen and began to turn it over and over. "Yeah. All boys."

She could have sworn that the baby in the photo she'd found in the desk had been a girl. "I suppose when you live somewhere as cold as Alaska, you have to find creative ways to keep warm."

"True, but constant procreating seems pretty extreme to me."

Hannah let out a laugh, but it died on her lips when she noticed his obvious uneasiness. "I was hoping you might introduce me to some more Lassiters."

He loosened his tie, a sure sign of discomfort. "It's ' :en crazy busy around here."

Like she really believed that after he'd told her his schedule happened to be light this week. "Are you sure you haven't been avoiding me?"

He turned his attention back to the pen. "Not intentionally. I'm sorry that I haven't spent much time with you."

So was she. "Anyway, that's not exactly why I'm here. I came upon something at the library this morning that I found interesting." She dug through her bag and withdrew the copy of the archived article, then slid it across the desk. "This is a picture of J.D. and his brother, Charles, at a rodeo here in Cheyenne over thirty years ago. Charles won the roping competition."

Logan studied it a few moments before regarding Hannah again. "And?"

She reached across the desk and pointed at the text below the photo. "Look at the list of winners."

Logan scanned the text before looking up, sheer surprise in his expression. "Your mother was a barrel racer?"

"Yes, she was, but she gave it up after I was born." Only one more thing Ruth had blamed on her daughter. "Now I'm wondering if she met J.D. through his brother during one of these competitions."

Logan seemed to mull that over for a moment. "I planned to question Marlene Lassiter about J.D.'s past. They were very close, so she might know something about an affair."

"I'd appreciate that, Logan." She would also appreciate a better explanation for his behavior the other night in the media room. "Now that we've settled this matter, we do need to move on to our other issue."

"What issue would that be?"

She refused to let him play dumb. "The one involving our attraction to each other, and your concerns that I don't know my own mind."

"Hannah, I'm worried that—"

"I'll have regrets…I know. You're worried I'm going to get hurt. But as I told you during our last conversation, I don't have any expectations. I don't need poetry or candy or any promises. I only want to enjoy your company while I'm here, whatever that might involve."

"I don't want to do anything to hurt you."

Time to set him straight. "I'm not some fragile little flower who needs to be sheltered from life, both the good and the bad."

"I never thought of you as fragile, Hannah. But you have to know that I'm not in the market to settle down and have a family."

How well she understood that. "Fine. I get that. I'll hold off on picking out the engagement ring. Now I have a question for you."

"Shoot."

She scooted to the edge of her chair and stared at him straight on. "Do you still want me?"

He tossed the pen aside. "You really have to ask that?"

"Yes, and I want an answer."

When he rolled the chair back and stood, Hannah expected one of two things—Logan was going to kiss her, or show her to the door. Instead, he walked to a control panel mounted on the wall, pushed a button and lowered the electronic blinds, securing their complete privacy. Then he moved in front of her chair, clasped her wrists to pull her into his arms and delivered a kiss so soft and sensual, she thought her knees might not hold her. As if he sensed her dilemma, he turned her around and lifted her onto the desk.

Her skirt rode up too high to be considered ladylike, but frankly she didn't care. She was too focused on the feel of Logan's palms on her thighs, the strokes of his thumbs on the inside of her legs that seemed timed with the silken glide of his tongue against hers. *Higher,* she wanted to tell him. *Please,* she almost pleaded. But before she could voice her requests, he broke the kiss.

"Are you convinced I still want you, Hannah?"

This time she decided to play dumb in hopes he'd make more attempts at persuading her. "Almost."

"Maybe this will help." He took her palm and pressed it against his erection, showing her clear evidence of his need.

"I'm convinced." And veritably panting.

He placed her hand back into her lap. "Do you know what I really want right now?"

Hopefully the same thing she wanted—for him to have his very wicked way with her on top of his desk. "Do tell."

"Lunch."

Clearly the man was bent on driving her straight into oblivion. "Are you serious?"

Logan lifted her off the desk and set her on her feet. "Dead serious. There's a café right down the street that serves great burgers where we can eat and talk. I've been meaning to take you there."

Hannah wanted him to just take her. Now. But a talk was definitely warranted. She sent a pointed look in the direction of his fly. "Are you sure you're up to it? Oh, wait. Obviously you are."

He let go a boisterous laugh. "You'll need to walk in front of me for a few minutes. Just don't shake your butt."

Oh, how tempting to do that very thing. Instead, she picked up her purse and took her time applying more lip gloss. After she popped the cap back on and dropped the tube into her bag, she smiled. "Are you recovered now?"

"Enough to retain my dignity, so let's get out of here before I change my mind, lock the door and tell Priscilla to hold all calls while I hold you captive for a few more hours."

"Promises, promises," Hannah teased as they walked into the hall and started toward the lobby.

When they rounded the corner, an attractive sixty-something, brown-haired woman wearing a tasteful red tailored coat dress, nearly ran head-on into Hannah. "I'm so sorry, honey," she said. "I shouldn't be in such a hurry."

"You're always in a hurry, Marlene."

She patted Logan's cheek and smiled. "Not any more than you are, young man. Particularly the other evening when you rushed out of my house like your hair was on fire."

Hannah sent a quick glance at Logan, then returned her attention to the first Lassiter she'd encountered thus far.

Logan moved behind Hannah and braced his palms on her shoulders. "Hannah, this is Marlene Lassiter. Marlene, Hannah Armstrong."

The woman gave her an odd look before she formed a tentative smile and offered her hand. "It's nice to finally meet you."

Hannah accepted the brief shake, but she couldn't quite accept that the woman found the situation nice at all. "And it's a pleasure to finally meet you, too. Logan has told me a lot of good things about you."

"Well, you can't believe everything he says," Marlene added with a sincere smile directed at Logan.

"Were you here to see me, Marlene?" Logan asked.

"No," she said. "I'm having lunch with Walter, provided he's ready to go. The man still works like a field hand when he should be considering retirement."

The sparkle in Marlene's eyes, and the telling comment, led Hannah to believe the couple must know each other beyond any business arrangements. "I suppose that comes with the territory."

Marlene fiddled with the diamond necklace at her throat. "Yes, I suppose it does. And I better see if I can hurry him along."

"Again, it's nice to meet you," Hannah said as Marlene hurried past them.

"You, too, Hannah," she said over one shoulder before disappearing into the office at the end of the hall.

Hannah and Logan remained silent until they exited and stepped foot onto the sidewalk, where Logan turned to Hannah. "I suspect there's a story there with Walter and Marlene."

Considering Marlene's uneasy expression when they met, Hannah wondered if the woman might actually know the story of her life.

Before Logan could open the glass door to the Wild Grouse Café, a brown-haired man walked out, blocking the path. At first he didn't recognize him, until he realized the guy happened to be a client, a premiere chef, and the second Lassiter he'd encountered that day. "Are you checking out the competition, Dylan?"

"Hey, Logan," he said with a smile as he shook Logan's offered hand. "Actually, I grabbed a bite here because it's still one of the best eateries in town, at least until the grand opening of our newest restaurant. I've barely had time to eat since I've been working on grabbing some good press for this venture to circumvent the bad press over the will dispute."

Bad press compliments of Dylan's sister, Angelica. "I hear you on the bad press, and finding time to eat. I'm actually going to have lunch for a change."

"So they do let you out of the law cage?"

"It happens now and then." When he remembered Hannah was behind him, he caught her arm and drew her forward. "Dylan, this is Hannah Armstrong. Hannah, this is Dylan Lassiter, CEO of the Lassiter Grill Corporation, a veritable restaurant empire."

Dylan grinned. "Pleased to meet you. And where have you been hiding her out, Whittaker?"

"I'm his maid," Hannah said as she returned his smile.

Dylan frowned. "Seriously?"

Leave it to Hannah to throw out a comeback, but then he'd really begun to appreciate her easy wit. "She's a teacher during the day."

"And Logan actually moonlights as a plumber," she said.

They exchanged a smile and a look over their inside joke, interrupted by Dylan clearing his throat. "Logan, as a word of warning, I just had lunch with my sister. She's still loaded for bear over the will, in case you want to reconsider and find somewhere else to dine."

Great. Another Lassiter, and this one wasn't going to be pleasant. "I can handle Angelica." As long as he used kid gloves. He just hoped she wasn't wearing boxing gloves.

Dylan slapped him on the back. "Good luck, Whittaker. And it was damn good to see you again. Nice to meet you, too, Hannah."

After Dylan rushed away, Logan escorted Hannah into the restaurant and walked up to the hostess stand to request a table. He glanced across the crowded dining room and immediately spotted Angelica Lassiter sitting alone, wearing a white tailored business suit and a major scowl. Unfortunately, she spotted him as well. Too late to turn tail and run, he realized, when she slid out of the booth and approached him at a fast clip.

She bore down on him like a Texas tornado, her dark hair swaying and brown eyes flashing. "Logan Whittaker, you didn't return my last call."

An intentional oversight, not that he'd tell her. "I've been busy, Angelica, and you should address all questions regarding the will to Walter."

"Walter won't listen to me," she said. "He keeps saying there's nothing I can do to change the paltry percentage of Lassiter Media I inherited and I should learn to live with the fact Evan controls the majority of the shares, and the voting power that affords him. I still can't believe Daddy did this to me."

Frankly, neither could Logan. Nor could he believe how Angelica, a strong, independent businesswoman, reportedly the spitting image of her mother, could sound so much like a lost little girl. "I'm sure he had his reasons, and I know they don't seem logical or fair. All I can say is hang in there."

This time Hannah stepped forward on her own volition. "Hi, I'm Hannah Armstrong, a friend of Logan's."

Angelica gave Hannah's offered hand a gentle shake and presented a pleasant smile. "It's truly a pleasure to meet one of Logan's friends. Perhaps we can have dinner at some point in time."

"I'd like that." And she would, for reasons she

couldn't even reveal—namely this woman could actually be her sister.

Angelica turned back to Logan. "I'm asking you as a friend to talk to Walter and see if I can somehow contest the will. That company should be mine, not Evan's." And with that she was gone as quickly as she'd come, fortunately for Logan and for Hannah.

Once they were seated across from each other in the booth Angelica had just vacated, Hannah folded her hands on the table before her. "What were the odds I'd meet two of J.D.'s offspring in one day?"

Slim to none. "Now that you have met them, what do you think?"

She seemed to mull over that query for a minute. "Well, Dylan seemed nice enough, and so did Angelica, although she did seem pretty angry. I assume it had something to do with the breakup and that will dispute that I came across in a newspaper article. Am I right?"

He wasn't at liberty to hand her all the dirty details. "That's part of it. But just so you know, she's actually a very nice woman. Smart and savvy and she spends a lot of time involved in charity work."

"Don't forget she's very pretty," Hannah added.

"Yeah, you could say that." And he'd probably said too much.

"Have you dated her?" Hannah asked, confirming his conjecture.

"No. She's ten years younger and not my type."

She braced her bent elbow on the table and propped her cheek on her palm, reminding him of that first night they'd had dinner together. "Exactly what is your type?"

Hard to say, other than she seemed to be fitting the

bill just fine. "Keen intelligence, a nice smile. Green eyes. And most important, a smart-ass sense of humor."

Hannah leaned back and laid a dramatic hand above her heart. "I do declare, Mr. Whittaker. You sure have high standards."

He narrowed his eyes. "And you're getting a Texas accent."

"I wonder why." She went from smiling to serious in less than a heartbeat. "It's really hard for me to believe the people I met today could be my half siblings. And it makes me angry that my mother withheld vital information years ago, preventing me from making my own decision whether or not to connect with them."

If she only knew the vital information he'd been withholding from her, she wouldn't be too thrilled with him, either. But little by little, he'd begun to think he could trust her enough to tell her about his own sorry past. Eventually. "If you did decide to sign the nondisclosure, you'd never have a chance to get to know them. And since you're determined not to sign it, you really should give getting to know them a shot."

Hannah pondered that statement for a few moments before speaking again. "That's an option I'm not ready to explore. And signing the nondisclosure waiver would be the price I'd pay if I claimed my inheritance."

He wondered if she'd come to her senses and changed her mind. "Are you reconsidering taking the money?"

She shook her head. "No. Although it's tempting, I still don't feel I can claim it in good conscience, or sign the nondisclosure. Knowing the annuity will be turned over to charity does make my decision much easier."

She didn't sound all that convincing to Logan. "You

still have some time to think it through before you have to leave." And he wasn't looking forward to her leaving, though he had no right whatsoever to ask her to stay.

After finishing their food, they engaged in casual conversation, covering movies and music they liked, before their discussion turned to Hannah's child. Logan listened intently while Hannah verbally demonstrated her devotion to her daughter. Not a day had gone by when he hadn't thought about his own daughter, Gracie, and what she would look like now at age twelve. If she'd be chasing boys, or chasing cows with her grandpa. If she'd be smart as a whip like her mom, and love all things horses like him. The signs had pointed to that equine love, but he'd never known for sure, and never would. Gracie had only ridden Lucy one time, and that was a shame on many counts. A mare that willing and able and gentle should be ridden more often....

"Did I lose you somewhere, Logan?"

His thoughts scattered and disappeared after Hannah made the inquiry. "Sorry. I just came up with a really good idea." And he had. A banner idea.

"What would that be?" she asked.

He stood, held out his hand and helped her out of the booth. "I'm going to take the rest of the day off and we're going to have some fun."

"What, pray tell, do you have in mind, Mr. Whittaker?"

"Sweetheart, we're going to take a long, long ride."

Seven

This wasn't at all what Hannah expected when Logan mentioned going for a ride. She'd envisioned satin sheets and afternoon delight in his bedroom that she had yet to see. She *hadn't* expected to be sitting atop a plodding mare that kept stopping to graze as they headed toward the creek.

"You're doing fairly well for someone who hasn't been on a horse for a while."

She shot him a withering look. "Remind me of that when I have a sore butt for the next few days."

Logan's rich, deep laugh echoed across the pastureland. "Nothing a good soak in the tub won't cure. Or a massage."

"Know a good massage therapist?"

That question brought a frown to Logan's face. "Why would you need one when you have me?"

Her day suddenly brightened significantly, along with the sun. "Are you good at giving massages?"

"So I've been told."

She didn't care to ask who had told him. "That's nice to know in case I do need your services."

He winked. "Oh, you're going to need them all right. And I promise you're going to enjoy them."

"I'm counting on you to make good on that promise." And counting on herself not to let her heart get tangled up in him. Of course, that would be easier said than done.

They continued to ride in companionable silence, and after traveling over most the surrounding land, Logan finally dismounted in one smooth move a little farther away from where they'd stood the other night. Hannah did the same with much less poise, grabbed the reins and tugged a single-minded Lucy in Logan's direction before the mare launched into another grass attack. "Why did we stop?"

Logan guided the gelding to the gate opening up to the pasture that led to the creek. "I want to show you another special place."

"Good," Hannah replied. "My bottom was just about to give out."

After leading the horses through the gate, Logan turned and closed it, then said, "Let Lucy go for now."

As predicted, the mare went to the nearest clump of grass. "She's a regular chow hound."

"She needs to be ridden more often," Logan said as he detached a rolled blanket from the back of his saddle and tucked it beneath his left arm. "We can take another ride this weekend on my nearest neighbor's property. He has a larger spread and he told me to feel free to use it anytime."

Hannah's spirits plummeted when she realized she was set to leave in three days. "I plan to go home on Saturday."

He clasped her hand in his and gave it a gentle squeeze. "You can stay until Sunday."

She just might at that. One more day wouldn't matter to Cassie. If anything, her daughter might be disappointed to see her if it meant going back to her normal routine. "We'll see."

Logan guided her down the incline a hundred yards or so from the fence and stopped beneath a cottonwood tree not far from the narrow creek. He released her hand to spread the blanket over the ground. "I've been known to come here to think."

Hannah looked around the area, amazed at the absolute quiet. "It does seem to be a good place to clear your head."

"Among other things."

She turned to see Logan had already planted himself on the blanket, removed his boots and reserved a space beside him. "Take off your shoes and take a load off," he said.

She really wanted to remove more than her shoes. More like her clothes. And his. It had now been confirmed—she could star in her own made-for-TV movie about a very bad girl titled *Hannah and Her Outrageous Hormones*.

After she toed out of her sneakers, she dropped down next to Logan as a little flurry of butterfly nerves flitted around in her belly. "So are we going to meditate now?"

Logan's eyes appeared to grow darker in the shade, and undeniably more intense. "That's up to you."

With that, he brought her down onto the blanket in his arms, where she rested her head on his chest. They stayed that way for a time, the sound of his heart beating softly in Hannah's ear, his arm stroking her shoulder back and forth in a soothing rhythm.

She lifted her head to find him staring at the overhead branches. "Dollar for your thoughts. To account for inflation."

His smile made a short-lived appearance before he turned sullen again. "I was thinking how quickly life can change in one moment."

Hannah returned her head to his chest. "I know that all too well. One day you're sending the man you married off to work, the next you learn you'll never see him again."

"What exactly happened to him?" he asked. "If you don't mind talking about it."

She didn't mind, at least not now. "He was rewiring a commercial building that was under renovation and something went wrong. After the electrocution, they rushed him to the hospital and tried everything they could to save him, but it was too late."

"Does anyone know what went wrong now?"

"At first the insurance company claimed Danny was at fault, but his coworkers said he did everything he should have been doing in accordance with the wiring diagram. So they offered me a two-hundred-thousand-dollar settlement and I took it."

"You should have sued them."

Spoken like an attorney. "With a baby on the way and a new mortgage, I couldn't afford to ride it out, possibly for years, or risk losing the suit and ending up with nothing. Danny had a small insurance policy, but it barely covered funeral expenses, let alone any hospital bills I incurred after having Cassie."

"And your mother couldn't help out financially?"

A cynical laugh slipped out before she could stop it. "She always acted as if she didn't have a dime. However, she gifted us the down payment on our house out of the blue. I was able to repay her in a manner of speaking when I took care of her after her cancer diagnosis."

"You did that and attended school?" he asked, his voice somewhat incredulous.

"She only lasted two more months during the summer, so I wasn't in school." Hannah thought back to that time and the bittersweet memories. "Funny, I always felt as if I'd been a burden to her because she was so unhappy and bitter. Yet the day before she died, she told me thank you, and said she loved me. I don't recall her telling me that the entire time I was growing up. She was never the demonstrative type."

He released a rough sigh. "I can't imagine a parent not telling a child they loved them. But maybe she was so consumed by anger over being jilted by your father, she couldn't see what a gift she had in you."

Hannah's heart panged in her chest. "I don't know about being a gift, but I tried my best to be a good girl so I could win her approval. Unfortunately it never seemed to be enough."

He gave her a gentle squeeze. "As hard as it was, her attitude probably made you a stronger person. Definitely a good person. One of the best I've met in a long time."

He was saying all the right things, and he'd said

them with sincerity. "You're kind of remarkable yourself."

"Don't kid yourself, Hannah. I'm just an average guy who's made more than my share of mistakes."

Those mystery mistakes he had yet to reveal, leaving Hannah's imagination wide open. "Haven't we all screwed up a time or two, Logan? You just have to learn from those mistakes and move on. And eventually you have to stop blaming yourself for your shortcomings. That was fairly hard for me."

"Why were you blaming yourself?"

She truly hated to drudge that up, but soul-cleansing seemed to be the order of the day. "The morning Danny died, I got on him about leaving his shoes on the living room floor and missing the clothes hamper. I should have said I loved him, but the last words he heard from me had to do with cleanliness. I can count on one hand the times I didn't say I loved him before he left for work."

He brushed a kiss over her forehead. "You had no way of knowing he wouldn't be coming home."

If only she had known. "I finally acknowledged that, but it didn't lessen the guilt for a long time. If it hadn't been for Gina verbally kicking my butt, I might still not be over it."

"She's a good friend, huh?"

The very best and one of the few people she'd trust with her child. "Yes, she is. Granted, she does like to throw out advice whether I ask or not."

"How does she feel about you being here with me?"

She thought it best to hand him the abridged version. "Oh, she's all for it. In fact, if she'd had her way, we would've been having wild monkey sex from the minute I walked through your door."

"That would've worked for me."

She looked up to see his grin and poked him in the side. "That's rich coming from the guy who left me high and dry in his home theater."

"Believe me, that wasn't an easy decision."

Revelation time. "Just so you know, the way you make me feel…well…I thought I might never feel that way again."

He tipped her chin up and said, "That's my goal right now, to make you—" he kissed her forehead "—feel—" he kissed her cheek "—real good."

When Logan finally moved to her mouth, all Hannah's pent-up desire seemed to come out in that kiss, a hot meeting of tastes and tongues and mingled breath. Soon they were not only lip-to-lip, but also facing each other body-to-body until Logan nudged Hannah onto her back. He kissed the side of her neck as he slid his calloused hand beneath her T-shirt, at first breezing up her rib cage until he found her breasts. When he kissed her thoroughly again, he also circled her nipple with his fingertip through the lacy bra, and she reacted with an involuntary movement of her hips. Dampness began to gather in a place too long neglected, and she felt as if she might spontaneously combust due to the heat his touch was generating.

Her breathing, as well as her pulse, sped up as he skimmed his palm down her belly. She would swear her respiration stopped when he slipped the button on her jeans and then slid the zipper down.

Logan left her lips and softly said, "Lift up," and when Hannah answered his command, he pushed her pants down to her thighs, leaving her brand-new, leopard-skin panties intact.

For a few minutes, he seemed determined to keep her in suspended animation, toying with the lace band below her navel without sliding his hand inside the silk, no matter how badly Hannah wanted it. He finally streamed a fingertip between her thighs and sent it in a back-and-forth motion. He knew exactly how and where to touch her, but he only continued a brief time before he took his hand away. She responded with a somewhat embarrassing groan of protest, yet she soon discovered she had nothing to complain about when Logan worked her panties down to join her jeans.

From that moment forward, every bit of her surroundings seemed to disappear. The only sound she heard happened to be Logan whispering sensual words in her ear about what he wanted to do to her, what she was doing to him right then. Some of the comments could be considered crude, but she regarded them as the sexiest phrases she'd ever heard. He knew all the right buttons to push and, boy, did he push them well. The pressure began to mount, bringing with it pure pleasure on the heels of an impending climax, compliments of Logan's gentle, right-on-target strokes. And when the orgasm hit all too soon, Hannah inadvertently dug her nails into his upper arm and battled a scream bubbling up from her throat.

She'd never been a screamer. She'd never been in a pasture with her pants down around her knees either, being tended to by one outrageously gorgeous, sexy guy who knew exactly how to treat a woman.

Hannah was suddenly consumed by the overwhelming need to have him inside her. Yet when she reached for his fly, he clasped her wrist to stop her. "Not here," he said. "Not now. This was all for you."

She focused on his beautiful face, the deep indentations framing his mouth. "But—"

"It's okay, sweetheart. I'm going to be fine until we get back to the house."

She lifted her head slightly, with effort, to look at him. "What are we going to do when we get there?"

"I'm going to show you my bed." He favored her with a grin. "That is, if you want to see it."

Who was he kidding? "I seriously thought you would never ask."

Logan could have gone with spontaneity, but he wanted this first time between them to be special. More importantly, he needed Hannah to know she meant more to him than a quick roll on the ground, instant gratification, then over and out. She'd begun to mean more to him than she probably should.

Taking her by the hand, he led her into the master bedroom and closed the door behind them, determined to shut out the world and any lingering reservations.

Hannah remained silent when he tossed back the covers then guided her to the side of the bed. "Take off your shoes." And that would be the last thing she'd remove by herself if he had any say in the matter, which he did.

While she sat on the edge of the bed and took off her sneakers, he sat in the adjacent chair to pull off his boots. Once that was done, he lifted her from the bed and back onto her bare feet. He saw absolute trust in her eyes after he pulled the T-shirt over her head and tossed it aside. He noticed some self-consciousness in her expression as he removed her bra, and unmistakable heat when he slid her jeans and panties to the floor. She braced one hand on his shoulder for balance as she stepped out of the remaining clothes, a slight blush on her cheeks when he swept her up and laid her on the bed.

The sun streamed in from the open curtains covering the windows facing the pasture, casting Hannah's beautiful body in a golden glow. He needed to touch her. Had to touch her. But first things first.

Her gaze didn't waver as Logan stripped off his shirt, but she did home in on the ink etched in his upper arm. He'd have to explain that later. Right then he had more pressing issues. After shoving down his jeans and boxer-briefs, he opened the nightstand drawer, withdrew a packet and tossed it onto his side of the bed. He returned his attention to Hannah, who looked more than a little interested in his erection, her eyes wide with wonder.

She caught his glance and smiled. "I didn't realize you were that happy to see me."

Happier than he'd been in a long, long time. "I'm ecstatic to be here."

"So am I."

Relieved to hear that confirmation, Logan claimed the empty space beside Hannah and remained on his knees to allow better access. As he slid his fingertip between her breasts, pausing to circle each nipple, then moved down her torso, Hannah's breath caught. And when he replaced his hand with his mouth to retrace his path, he would swear she stopped breathing altogether.

When it came to sex, the advantage always went to women—they required little to no recovery time. And although his own body screamed for release, he was bent on proving that fact.

Logan nudged her legs apart to make a place for himself, then planted a kiss right below her navel. He didn't linger there long because he had somewhere more interesting to go. An intimate place that needed tending. When his mouth hit home, Hannah jerked from the impact. But he didn't let up, using his tongue to tease her into another climax. And as far as he could tell, this one was stronger than the last, apparent when she dug her nails even deeper into his shoulder.

He'd waited as long as physically possible to make love to her completely, and that sent him onto his back to reach for the condom. In a real big hurry, he tore the packet open with his teeth and had it in place in record time. He moved over her, eased inside her and called up every ounce of control to savor the feel of her surrounding him.

He'd learned long ago how to take a woman to the limits, but he also learned how to shelter his emotions in recent years. His sexual partners—and they'd been very few and far between—had been a means to an end. No commitments. No promises. Only mutual physical satisfaction. Up to that moment, he hadn't realized how empty his life had become. Until Hannah.

He minimized his movements as he held her closely. He wanted it to last, if not forever, at least a little while longer. But nature had other ideas, and the orgasm crashed down on him with the force of a hurricane.

Logan couldn't remember the last time he'd shaken so hard, or the last time his heart had beaten so fast. He sure as hell couldn't recall wanting to remain that way for the rest of the day, in the arms of someone he'd known for such a short while. But at times, he'd felt as if he'd known Hannah for years.

When she moved slightly beneath him and sighed, he took that as a cue his weight might be getting to her. But after he shifted over onto his back, she asked, "Where are you going?"

He slid his arm beneath her and brought her against his side. "I'm still here, Hannah."

She rose up and traced one half of the broken-heart tattoo on his upper arm, etched with an *A* on one side, and a *G* on the other. "Are these your ex-wife's initials?"

He'd expected that question, and he decided on a half-truth. "No. They belong to a girl I used to know." His baby girl.

She rested her cheek on his chest, right above his heart, which was pounding for a different reason now. "She must have been very special, and I'm sorry she broke your heart."

After another span of silence passed, Logan thought she'd fallen asleep. She proved him wrong when she asked, "You've never really considered having children of your own?"

Alarm bells rang in his head. "I'm not cut out for fatherhood."

She raised her head again and stared at him. "How could you possibly know that if you haven't even tried it? Or do you just not like kids?"

"I like kids a lot. They're way the hell more honest than adults. But it takes more than liking a child to raise them right."

She settled back on the pillow. "I personally think you'd be good at it, for what it's worth."

In a moment of clarity, Logan realized Hannah deserved the truth. She had to know the real man behind the facade. It pained him to think about reliving those details. He'd be tearing open an old wound that still refused to heal. He also could be inviting her scorn, and that would be even worse. Still, he felt he had no choice but to be open and honest.

"Hannah?"

"Hmmm…" she murmured as she softly stroked his belly.

"There's something I need to tell you, and it's not going to be pretty."

Hannah sensed he'd been concealing a secret all along, but was she prepared to hear it? She certainly better be, she realized, when Logan handed her the T-shirt and panties, then told her to put them on with a strange detachment that belied the sadness in his brown eyes.

While she dressed, Logan pulled on his jeans before sitting on the bed's edge and turning his back to her. A long period of silence passed and for a minute she wondered if he'd reconsidered confessing whatever it was he felt the need to confess.

"I had a daughter at one time."

Hannah bit back an audible gasp. She'd expected an affair, a business deal gone bad. Maybe even bankruptcy, although that didn't make much sense considering he'd purchased a million-dollar home. But she could not have predicated he'd lied about being a father. Then again, that could explain the framed photo she'd found in his desk drawer. "Did you lose custody?"

"I lost her because she died."

And Hannah only thought she couldn't be more stunned. "When did this happen, Logan?"

"Almost eight years ago," he said in a weary tone. "She was only four years old."

She swallowed around her shock right before her

ability to relate to his loss drew her to his side. She laid a hand on his shoulder. "I'm so sorry, Logan." It was all she could think to say at a moment like this. Now she understood why so many people had been at a loss for words following Danny's death.

He leaned forward, hands clasped over his parted knees as he kept his eyes trained on the dark hardwood floor beneath his feet. "Her name was Grace Ann. I called her Gracie."

The truth behind the tattoo. Devastating loss had broken his heart. Not a woman, but a precious child. "I know how badly it hurts to lose a husband, but I can't even begin to imagine how difficult it would be to lose a child."

"That's because it's unimaginable until it happens to you." His rough sigh echoed in the deathly quiet room. "When Jana got pregnant, we'd barely been out of law school. We were both ambitious and career-minded. A kid hadn't been a part of the plan. But when Gracie was born, and they put that tiny baby girl in my arms, I thought I'd be terrified. Instead, I was totally blown away by how much I loved her at that moment. How I would've moved mountains to keep her safe. And I failed to do that."

Hannah desperately wanted to ask for details, but she didn't want to push him. "Things happen, Logan. Horrible things that we can't predict or prevent."

"I could have prevented it."

Once more Hannah didn't know how to respond, so she waited until he spoke again. *If* he spoke again.

A few more seconds passed before he broke the pain-filled silence. "I bought her one of those little bikes for her fourth birthday. The kind that still had training wheels. She loved that bike." He paused as if lost in the memories before he continued. "A couple of days later, I was supposed to be home early to help her learn to ride it. I'd just made junior partner, and I was assigned the case of a lifetime that would've netted the firm a windfall. The pretrial hearing went on longer than expected that afternoon, so I wasn't going to make it home before dark. My job took precedence over my daughter."

The guilt in his tone was instantly recognizable to Hannah. "You're not the first man to put work over family when the situation calls for it. Danny missed dinner many times because he had to put in overtime to secure our future."

"But I had earned plenty of money by then, and so had my wife. I could have turned the hearing over to the associate working the case with me, but I was so damn driven to prove the senior partners had been justified in choosing me over two other candidates. And that drive cost my child her life."

She truly needed to know what had happened, but did she dare ask? "Logan, I'm really trying to understand why you feel you're to blame, but I'm having some problems with that with so little information to go on."

Logan glanced at her again before returning his focus to the floor. "When I drove up that night, I saw the ambulance and police cruiser parked in front of the house. I tried to tell myself one of the neighborhood teens had been driving too fast and had had an accident. But my gut told me something inconceivable had happened, and it turned out I was right." He drew in a ragged breath and exhaled slowly. "I pulled up to the curb, got out of the car and started toward the ambulance, only to be met by an officer who told me not to go any farther. He said Grace had ridden the bike into the street and a woman driving by didn't see her, and she didn't even have time to put on her brakes."

Hannah felt his anguish as keenly as if it were her own. "Oh, Logan, I don't know what to say." And she honestly didn't. Again.

"Her death was instant, they told me," he said, as if he couldn't stop the flow of words. "She didn't suffer. But we all suffered. My marriage definitely suffered. Jana screamed at me that night and told me she'd never forgive me."

That threw Hannah for a mental loop. "She blamed you?"

He forked both hands through his hair. "We blamed each other. She blamed me for the bike and not being at a home on time. I blamed her for not watching Gracie closely enough. We both blamed the nanny for leaving early."

While Hannah pondered all she had learned, Logan went silent for a few more seconds before he released a ragged breath. "We had an alarm on the pool," he said. "We bought a top-rate security system and had every inch of the house child-proofed. But it wasn't enough. It came down to one unlocked door to the garage and Gracie climbing on a step stool to open the garage door, and she'd never been a climber."

Hannah had one burning question she had to ask. "Where was your wife at the time Gracie left the house?"

"Checking her email. She said Gracie was watching a DVD in the den only minutes before she went into the home office, and I had no reason not to believe her. Jana had always been a good mother, even if she had the same drive to succeed as I did. Basically, a few minutes of inattentiveness on Jana's part, and blind ambition on my part, irreparably changed our lives forever."

To Hannah, Logan's wife seemed more at fault than he did. But then she really couldn't completely blame her when she had been guilty of the same inattentiveness. "Children can be natural-born escape artists, no matter how vigilant the parent. Cassie got away from me in the grocery store once when I wasn't paying attention to her. It took a half hour and a security guard to find her. I was lucky someone didn't kidnap her when it would have been so easy."

"Gracie knew better than to leave the house without an adult," he said. "Until that night, she never had. I should have suspected she might pull something with the bike when I talked to her that afternoon."

"You spoke to Gracie?"

He smiled a sad smile that shot straight to Hannah's heart. "Yeah. I called Jana to say I was going to be late and she put Gracie on the phone so I could explain. When I told her I couldn't help her ride the bike that night, she was mad as a wet hen and told me she'd do it herself. I said that wasn't allowed and if she tried it, I'd take the bike away. She pouted for a few minutes but when I promised to help her the next day, and take her to the zoo that weekend, she seemed happy enough. Her last words to me were 'I love you, Daddy Bear.' She had a thing for Goldilocks."

Hannah's eyes began to mist like morning fog. "I know it's not the same thing as having her in your life, but at least you'll always have Gracie's wonderful last words to keep in your memory bank."

"But it's never been enough," he said, his voice

hoarse with emotion. "I finally did forgive Jana, but it was too little, too late. And when it came right down to it, she'd been right. I never should have bought Gracie the damn bike."

A solid stretch of logic, but logic didn't count for much when it came to guilt and grief. "When are you going to forgive yourself, Logan?"

He looked at her as if she'd presented a totally foreign concept. "Forgiveness is earned, Hannah. I'm not there yet."

She wanted to inquire as to how long it might take before he reached that point, but he looked completely drained. "I can tell you're tired." Of the conversation and the pain.

He swept both hands over his face. "I'm exhausted."

Hannah stretched out on her back on the bed and opened her arms to him. "Come lie down with me for a little while."

For a split second she thought he might ignore her request, but instead he shrugged out of his jeans and surprisingly accepted the solace she offered.

Curled up together, they slept for a while, until the sun had been replaced by darkness. Logan made love to her again, at first slowly, gently, completely, before a certain desperation seemed to take over. "I can't get close enough," he said, even though they were as close as two people could be.

"It's okay," she kept telling him, until his body went rigid and he released a low moan.

In the aftermath, he brought his lips to her ear and whispered, "Stay with me, sweetheart."

She caressed his shadowed jaw and almost started to cry over the tenderness in his request. "I'm not going anywhere, Logan."

"I meant don't leave on Saturday. Stay another week."

Temptation came calling, but wisdom won out. "I need to get home to Cassie."

"I know I don't have any right to ask, but I need you to be here for a little longer."

I need you....

Those three powerful words shattered Hannah's resolve. Cassie would be fine without her for another week, perhaps even happy to have the extra time with her best friend, that much she knew. Gina would be okay with her extended stay as well.

Logan needed her, and it felt so good to be needed. She instinctively knew she couldn't save him, but maybe if she loved him enough...

Loved him? If she wasn't completely there, she was well on her way, perhaps to her own detriment. She might regret giving in to that emotion, but she would never regret knowing him or what they had shared. What they would share.

"All right, Logan. I'll stay."

Eight

"Logan Whittaker, what brings you all the way out here in the middle of the week and the middle of the day?"

A quest for information he sensed Marlene held. He'd revealed his sorry secrets to Hannah several days ago, and now he wanted Marlene to do the same. "I'm taking a late lunch. Guess I should have called first."

"Don't be silly," she said as she held open the door. "You're practically family."

After he stepped through the door, Marlene pointed to the doors leading to the outdoor entertainment area. "Since it's such a lovely day, let's talk outside," she said as she showed Logan onto the flagstone deck adjacent to the massive great room. He settled on a rattan chair while she took the one to his left.

The 30,000 acres comprising the Big Blue ranch

spread out before them as far as the eye could see. The original homestead where J.D. and Ellie Lassiter had raised their family, now occupied by Marlene's son, Chance, sat in the distance beneath the blue sky that inspired the ranch's name. He'd learned the history early on, but it had never impacted him like it did today. "I'd like to build a house on a place like this in the future. Far away from everything with no signs whatsoever of the city." No suburban streets where playing kids could get hurt, or worse, and that unexpected thought gave him pause. He didn't intend to have any more kids. Not now. Not ever.

"It is peaceful," Marlene said. "All the Lassiter children enjoyed living here."

Speaking of Lassiter children...

Logan glanced back and peered inside through the uncovered floor-to-ceiling windows, looking for signs of other life—namely J.D.'s only daughter. "Is Angelica staying here right now?" Not only did he not want a repeat of their last conversation, but he also didn't want to risk her accidentally overhearing that her own father had taken a mistress, and produced a child. That would categorically send her over the edge. Of course, that would only happen if Marlene came clean.

"Angelica is back in L.A. for a couple of days," she said. "And quite honestly, that's a good thing. That girl has been in a constant tizzy lately. She needs a break. *I* need a break."

"I totally understand. J.D.'s decisions on who inherits his millions have created a lot of questions." Especially for Hannah.

Marlene reached over and patted his arm. "Now why are you here, honey?"

A perfect lead-in to the reason for his impromptu visit. "It's actually about those aforementioned questions. I'm pretty sure you have information about Hannah Armstrong's parentage, namely her connection to J.D. And if you do know anything about that, tell me now because she has a right to know."

She began to wring her hands like an old-time washer. "It's probably past time Hannah learns the truth, and I do know the details. But I wouldn't feel right discussing those particulars with you before I speak with her."

His suspicions had been upheld, and the answers were within Hannah's grasp. A good thing for Hannah because she would know the truth. A bad thing for him because she'd have no reason not to return to Boulder immediately. But delaying the revelation would be selfish on his part. "If I bring her by, will you tell her the whole truth?"

Marlene raised a brow. "She's still here?"

"Yeah. I asked her to stay another week." An unforgettable week of lovemaking and conversation and making a connection with a woman who'd become very special to him. A week that had passed way too fast. But since he had so little to offer her, he would be forced to let her go eventually.

"What makes this one so different from the rest, Logan?" Marlene asked, cutting into his thoughts.

He could recite every one of Hannah's attributes, but that would take hours, so he chose to list only a few. "She's funny and kind but also damn tough. Not many people could handle losing a husband, raising a child on their own, caring for an ill parent and finishing college in the process. Without even trying, she also has the means to make a person want to tell their life story." Much like the woman sitting next to him.

She raised a brow. "Did you tell her yours?"

He streaked a palm over his neck. "Yeah. She knows about Grace." And it had almost killed him to tell her.

Marlene smiled a mother's smile. "I am so glad, Logan. And since she's still sticking around, I assume that she holds the opinion you're not to blame, like I do. Am I right?"

"Yeah, you are." Even if he still didn't agree with that lack of blame assumption. "But she's also compassionate."

"She's a woman who understands loss," Marlene said. "I do as well. We're all unwitting members of a club drawn together by that loss, and sadly that also includes you, too. Hannah intimately understands your pain, and you're very lucky to have found her."

"Don't read too much into this relationship. On Saturday, she's going back to her life and I'll go back to mine."

"Your currently lonely life?" She topped off the question with a frown. "You'd be a fool to let her go, Logan, when she could be a part of your future."

Here we go again. "We had this conversation last week."

"And we'll continue to have it until you listen to reason."

If that's the way she wanted to play it, he'd reiterate all the reasons why a permanent relationship wouldn't work with anyone, especially Hannah. "Marlene, my job doesn't allow for a personal life, and I don't intend to quit for another twenty years, if then."

"Work isn't everything," she said. "Family is."

His profession had indirectly destroyed one family. He wasn't going to risk that possibility again. "Look, I enjoy being with Hannah, but I'm not sure I'll ever be able to make a serious commitment again. I've already been through one divorce and I don't want a repeat. And most important, Hannah's a single mom. She's going to have expectations I might not be able to meet."

Marlene narrowed her eyes and studied him for a few moments. "Part of your reluctance has to do with her daughter, doesn't it?"

Only someone as astute as Marlene would figure that out. "Could you blame me for being concerned? What if I became close with Cassie and my relationship with Hannah doesn't work out? That would be like—"

"Losing Grace all over again?"

She'd hit that nail on the head. "It wouldn't be fair to either one of them."

Marlene leaned forward, keeping her gaze on his. "Honey, life is about balance and a certain amount of chance-taking when it comes to matters of the heart. But life without the possibility of love isn't really living at all. We aren't meant to be alone. Just keep that in mind before you dismiss Hannah due to your fears."

"I'm only afraid of hurting her, Marlene." Afraid he might fail Hannah the way he'd failed his former wife and daughter.

"Maybe you should let her decide if she wants to take a chance on you."

Needing a quick escape, Logan checked his watch and stood. "I have an appointment in less than an hour, so I better get back to the office. When do you want to have that talk with Hannah?"

Marlene came to her feet. "Bring her over for lunch

on Saturday. I'll take her aside after that and speak with her privately. Better still, why don't you bring her daughter, Cassie, too? You could surprise her as a Mother's Day gesture, and give yourself some extra time with her as well."

He'd totally forgotten about the holiday. Marlene's suggestion would buy him more time with Hannah, and he knew she would appreciate the gesture. "I'd have to figure out how I could manage that without her knowing."

Marlene patted his cheek. "You're a smart man, Logan. You'll come up with a plan."

And that plan suddenly began to formulate in his mind. Marlene's suggestion just might work after all. But could he deal with being around a little girl so close in age to Grace when he'd lost her? He wouldn't know unless he tried, and this time he needed to consider Hannah, not himself.

Logan gave Marlene a quick hug. "Thanks for doing this for Hannah. She really needs to know how she came to be."

"You're welcome, honey. And once she learns the whole truth, she's going to need you to lean on."

Being there for her, like she had been there for him, was pretty much a no-brainer. "She's already figured out J.D. was her father. You'll only ease her mind if you confirm it."

Marlene sighed. "On second thought, maybe it's better I provide you with some information first so you'll be prepared. As long as you promise not to say anything to her before I do."

He just wished she would make up her mind. "Fine,

as long as you tell me everything, down to the last detail."

"J.D. didn't father Hannah."

Apparently they'd been traveling straight down the wrong-information path. "Then who was it?"

"My husband, Charles."

She'd spent the day doing laundry and packing her clothes—her final day in Cheyenne.

When Logan sent her a text saying he'd be home by 3:00 p.m., Hannah waited for him on the great-room sofa, wearing only his white tailored button-down shirt. She felt somewhat foolish, but what better way to greet him on their last night together? Even after days of nonstop searching, tomorrow she would return home with no answers about her father and no idea if she would ever see Logan again.

He'd seemed somewhat distant the past two days, or at the very least distracted. She couldn't help but believe he'd been planning his goodbye, and she should be preparing for it now. As soon as she implemented her current and somewhat questionable plan, she would. In the meantime, she refused to think about the impending heartache brought on because she'd been naive enough to fall in love with a man who might never love her back.

Ten minutes later, when she heard the front door open, Hannah stretched out on the cushions on her side and struck what she hoped would be deemed a sexy pose. Logan strode into the room, tossed his briefcase aside and stopped dead in his tracks when he caught sight of her. "Howdy, ma'am."

She brushed her hair back with one hand and smiled. "Howdy yourself."

He walked up to the couch and hovered above her. "I have never said this to a woman before, but you're going to have to get dressed."

She pretended to pout. "You don't like what I'm wearing?"

"Oh, yeah," he said. "But I have a surprise for you and it requires that you put on some clothes."

She straightened and lowered her feet to the floor. "I have a surprise for you, too. I'm not wearing any panties."

He hesitated a moment, his eyes growing dark with that familiar desire. "We don't have a whole lot of time, and I need to take a shower."

Hannah slipped two buttons on the shirt, giving him a bird's-eye view of her breasts. "Imagine that. So do I. We could go green and do it together."

His resistance dissolved right before her eyes, and he proved he was no match for their chemistry when he clasped her hands and tugged her off the sofa. "Then let's go conserve some water."

They rushed through the house, pausing to kiss on the way to Logan's bedroom. Once there, they began to shed their clothes article by article, until they reached the bathroom, completely naked and needy.

He pressed a series of buttons on the nearby chrome panel, sending several showerheads set into the stone walls into watery motion.

While the digital thermostat adjusted the temperature, Hannah stood behind Logan, her arms wrapped around his bare waist. "If I use your soap and shampoo, I'm going to smell like a guy."

He turned her into his arms and grinned. "Better than me smelling like a girl. Of course, you could go get your stuff, but that would take time we don't have." He punctuated the comment by placing a palm on her bottom and nudging her against his erection.

What a man. A sexy, incredible man. "I get the point. Now don't just stand there, take me in the shower."

"That's precisely what I plan to do."

All talk ceased as they took turns washing each other with soap and shampoo that smelled like Logan—clean, not cologne-like. For all intents and purposes, Hannah didn't care if she carried the trace scent of him on her flesh all night, or back home with her tomorrow for that matter. She rejected all thoughts of leaving, and fortunately for her, Logan aided in that cause with his gentle caresses and persuasive kisses that he feathered down her body. He kneeled before her and brought her to the brink of climax with his mouth, then suddenly straightened and pressed the control that cut off the sprays.

His rapid breathing echoed in the large stone shower before he groaned the single word, "Condom."

Hannah did a mental calculation and realized it would be the worst time to take a chance. "We absolutely have to have one before we go any further."

"I know. Getting you pregnant is the last thing I need."

She couldn't deny that his firm tone stung a little, but she also acknowledged he had his reasons for being so resolute—he wanted no more children, period. "Should we take this to the bedroom?"

"Good idea."

They had barely dried off before Logan gathered her

up in his arms, carried her to the bedroom and didn't even bother to turn down the covers. He simply deposited her on the navy comforter and put the condom in place in record time, then faced her on the mattress, one arm draped over her hip.

"I want to really see you when we make love," he said, followed by a brief yet stimulating kiss.

With the room bathed in sunlight, Hannah didn't view that as an issue. "It's still daytime."

"I want you to be in charge."

She gave him an intentionally furtive grin. "You want me on top."

"You got it."

Not a problem, she thought, as she rose up and straddled his thighs. Quite an extraordinary fit, she realized after he lifted her up and guided himself inside her. From that moment on, instinct took over as Hannah took the lead. She suddenly felt as if she'd become someone else—a truly sensual being with the capacity to be completely in control. Yet that control began to wane as Logan touched her again and again, and didn't let up until the last pulse of her orgasm subsided. Only then did she realize he was fairly close to losing it, and she took supreme advantage, using the movement of her hips to send him over the edge. She watched in wonder as the climax began to take hold. His respiration increased, his jaw locked tight and he hissed out a long breath as his body tensed beneath her, yet he never took his gaze from hers.

Feeling physically drained, Hannah collapsed against Logan's chest and rested her head against his pounding heart. He gently rubbed her back with one hand and stroked her hair with the other, lulling her into a total sense of peace.

After a time, he rolled her over onto her back, remained above her and touched her face with a reverence that almost brought tears to her eyes. "You're phenomenal, sweetheart."

But not phenomenal enough to figure into his future. "You're not so bad yourself, sexy guy."

She took his ensuing smile to memory to bring back out on a rainy day. "I wish…" His words trailed off, along with his gaze.

"You wish what?"

"I wish I'd met you years ago, back when we were both young and unattached."

Before his life had taken a terrible turn, she assumed. "Well, since you're eight years older, and I married at the ripe old age of twenty, that would have made me jailbait if you'd dated me before I met Danny."

"I guess you're right about that, and from what I gather, you loved your husband very much."

"I did," she said without hesitation. "But I also know he'd want me to be happy and go on with my life."

He turned onto his back and draped an arm over his forehead. "You deserve to be happy, Hannah. And someday you're going to find someone who will do that for you."

Clearly he believed he didn't qualify, when in truth he did. Not exactly goodbye, but pretty darn close.

She sat up and scooted to the edge of the bed so he wouldn't see the tears starting to form in her eyes.

"Hannah, are you okay?"

No, she wasn't. Not in the least. But she would be because she was a survivor. "I'm fine. I just thought

I'd get dressed since I do believe you mentioned we have some place to be."

When she started to stand, Logan caught her wrist before she could come to her feet. "Believe me, if things were different, if I were the right man for you—"

She pivoted around to face him and faked a smile. "It's all right, Logan. I told you before this thing started between us I had no expectations where we're concerned." And, boy, had she lied without even realizing it.

"You're one in a million, Hannah, and never forget that."

One thing she knew to be true, she would never forget him.

An hour later, Hannah climbed into Logan's Mercedes and they set out for who knew where. She dozed off for a bit and awoke to find they were close to Fort Collins in Colorado, heading in the direction of Boulder.

She hid a yawn behind her hand before shooting a glance at Logan. "If you wanted me to go home, all you had to do was ask."

He gave her a quick grin before concentrating on the road. "That's not where we're going."

"Do you mind telling me were we *are* we going?"

"You'll see real soon."

Five minutes later, he exited the interstate and pulled into a rest stop, leading Hannah to believe Logan needed a break. He shut off the ignition, slid out of the sedan without saying a word, rounded the hood and then opened her door. "Time to get out and take a walk."

"I don't need a walk."

"You'll want to take this one whether you need it or not."

She tapped her chin and pretended to think. "Let me guess. You've arranged for an intimate dinner to be catered at a roadside park."

"Not hardly."

"A picnic beneath the halogen light set to the sights and sounds of eighteen-wheelers, complete with the smell of diesel fuel?"

He braced a hand on the top of the door. "You can sit there and crack jokes, or you can come and see your surprise."

She saluted like a practiced soldier. "Whatever you say, Your Excellency."

Hannah exited the car with Logan's assistance and followed behind him, completely confused over where he could be taking her. Then she saw the familiar silver SUV, the sweet, recognizable face pressed against the back window, and it all began to make sense.

Gina came around from the driver's side, opened the door and released a squealing redhead dressed in white sneakers, floral blue shorts and matching shirt, and of course the tiara planted on her head. "Mama!"

Hannah kneeled down and nearly fell over backward due to her daughter's voracious hug. "I missed you so much, sweetie!" she said as she showered Cassie's cheeks with kisses. "But what are you doing here?"

The little girl reared back, wiped her wet face and displayed her snaggletoothed grin. "It's an early Mother's Day gift. Gina told me I'm gonna spend the weekend with you and the prince!"

"And it was all His Royal Hotness's idea," her best

friend said as she approached carrying Cassie's suitcase and booster seat.

Hannah straightened and turned to Logan. "How did you manage to make this happen without my knowledge?"

He streaked a hand over his nape. "It took some work and some sneaking around. I had to steal your phone when you weren't looking so I could get Gina's number."

"Then he called and asked me to bring Cassie halfway," she added. "Now here we are and Frank's at home with a crying son and a pouting daughter who's mourning the temporary loss of her best gal pal."

Only a short while ago, Logan had claimed he couldn't be the kind of man she needed, and then he did something so wonderfully considerate and totally unselfish to prove himself wrong, wrong, wrong. "This is a very welcome surprise, Mr. Whittaker. Thank you very much."

He took the bag and seat from Gina. "You're very welcome."

Cassie tugged on Logan's shirt sleeve to garner his attention. "I'm hungry, Prince Logan."

"Then we should probably get on the road so we can get the queen something to eat." His follow-up bow brought back Cassie's vibrant grin.

Hannah took the suitcase from Logan's grasp. "If you don't mind getting her settled into the car, I'll be along in a minute right after I receive a full report from Gina." She then set her attention on her daughter. "And Cassie, stay close to Logan when you're crossing the parking lot."

"You can count on that," he said with all the determination of a man who believed he'd failed to protect his own little girl.

When Cassie slid her hand into Logan's hand, Hannah saw the flash of emotion in his eyes and she could picture how many memories had assaulted him in that moment. After they walked away—the cowboy attorney with the slow, easy gait, and the bouncing queen wannabe—she turned back to her friend. *"Your Hotness?* Really?"

Gina shrugged. "Seemed pretty appropriate to me."

"You know, I'd be mad at you over that comment if I didn't so appreciate everything you've done. Not only this evening, but over the past two weeks."

"The question is, Hannah, was it worth it? Did you finally find what you were looking for?"

She shook her head. "I still don't know who my father might be, and I've accepted the fact I might never know."

Gina rolled her eyes. "I don't mean only the thing with your long-lost dad. I'm referring to you and the lawyer. Do you see a future with him in it?"

Sadly, she didn't. "He's not the kind to settle down, Gina. He's a remarkable man who's been through a lot, but he's closed himself off emotionally. And that's okay. I didn't expect anything to come of it anyway."

Her friend nailed her with a glare. "You did it, didn't you?"

This time Hannah rolled her eyes. "We had this discussion at least three times last week and once this week. Yes, we did it. Often."

"I'm not talking about the sex," Gina said. "You've gone and fallen in love with him, haven't you? And don't hand me any bull because I can read it all over your face, you ninny."

Hannah's hackles came to attention. "I am not a ninny, and I didn't fall in love with him." Much.

"You lie like a cheap rug."

"You're too meddlesome for my own good." Hannah hooked a thumb over her shoulder. "My daughter is waiting for me."

Gina held up both hands, palms forward, as if in surrender. "Fine. Go with your daughter and the hunk. But when you get home tomorrow, we're going to have a long talk about the virtues of emotionally safe sex."

That worked for Hannah, and after that talk, she could very well need to have a long, long cry.

By the time they arrived home, Logan had been steeped in so many recollections, he'd begun to feel the burn of regret. Watching Cassie at the café ordering a kid's meal and coloring on the menu, he remembered Gracie at every turn. And he missed her. God, did he miss her.

The ache grew worse when he carried a sleeping Cassie up the stairs and to the second surprise of the evening.

"You can put her in my bed," Hannah said from behind him.

That wasn't a part of the plan. "She'll sleep better in here." He opened the door to the room he'd kept as a tribute to his own daughter.

Hannah gaped when she saw the double bed covered by a white comforter imprinted with pink slippers to match the décor. "When did you do this?" she whispered as she turned down the covers.

He laid Cassie carefully on the sheets, her thumb planted firmly in her mouth, her eyes still closed against the light coming from the lamp on the nightstand. "I'll tell you in a minute."

After Hannah pulled off her daughter's shoes, then gave her a kiss on the cheek, they walked back into the hall.

Logan closed the door and turned to her. "The owner of a furniture store in town happens to be a client. I arranged to have the bed delivered right after we got on the road tonight."

"And the bedspread?"

"I bought it yesterday during lunch." Another gesture that had rocked him to the core.

Hannah folded her arms beneath her breasts. "I don't mean to seem ungrateful, because I do appreciate your consideration. But my question is, why would you buy a bed when we're only going to be here one night?"

"I thought maybe you'd agree to stay another night."

She sighed. "I need to get home and resume my job search."

He started to grasp at hopeless straws. "Maybe you and Cassie could visit now and then when you have the chance. I could teach her to ride Lucy."

"What would be the point in that, Logan? You've already established this relationship isn't going to go anywhere. So why would I get my daughter's hopes up and lead her to believe there could be more between us?"

She evidently wanted him to say there could be more, and he couldn't in good conscience promise her that. "I guess you're right."

"Yes, I am right. Now that we've cleared that up,

I'm going to get ready for bed and I'll see you in the morning."

He shouldn't be surprised by her curt dismissal, since he'd made it perfectly clear earlier that he couldn't be the man in her life, but he hadn't expected this rejection to twist his gut in knots. However, despite his wounded male pride, he still could provide the information she'd sought from the beginning. "Marlene Lassiter wants us to have lunch at the Big Blue ranch tomorrow."

She frowned. "I really planned to get on the road early."

"Can you wait to leave until later?" he asked, trying hard not to sound like a desperate idiot. "The ranch is a great place for a kid to play. Cassie would enjoy it." He'd learned long ago if you wanted to melt a good mom's heart, you only had to mention her kids.

He realized the ploy had worked when she said, "I guess a few extra hours won't matter. Besides, I might grab the opportunity to ask Marlene a few questions about J.D., if you don't think I'd be overstepping my bounds."

She had no idea that's exactly what Marlene intended to do—answer all her questions—and he couldn't help but feel guilty over not being forthcoming with what he knew. "Actually, it's a real good idea. Since you haven't signed the nondisclosure, I'm sure she'd be willing to tell you what she knows."

"Provided she actually knows something."

Little did she know, tomorrow she would not only learn about her real father, she would also discover she had a brother. "You might be surprised."

"Probably not," she said. "But I guess I'll find out."

When she started away, he caught her hand and pulled her into his arms. She allowed it for only a moment before she tugged out of his hold and said, "Sleep well, Logan."

For the first time in several days, Hannah retired to her own bedroom, and Logan left for his, without even a kiss good-night.

Sleep well? No way. Not with the prospect of letting her go hanging over his head. But he still had another day in her presence. He would make it his goal to show her and her daughter a good time, and try one more time to convince himself why he didn't deserve her.

Nine

When Marlene Lassiter showed her into a private study at the main house for an after-lunch chat, Hannah could barely contain her curiosity. She wondered if perhaps the woman might hand her the third degree about her relationship with Logan. If so, Marlene would be encountering a major dead end with that one. Truth was, after today, the relationship would be null and void.

"Have a seat, dear," Marlene said as she gestured to one of two brown leather chairs before she crossed the room, nervously tugging at the back hem of her white cotton blouse that covered her black slacks.

After Marlene paused at what appeared to be a bar, Hannah took a seat and conducted a quick visual search of the room. The office was rustic and large, like the rest of the Lassiter family homestead, with bookcases flanking another stone fireplace. That fireplace was much smaller in scale than the one in the great room, where they'd left Logan watching some animated film with Cassie, who'd adhered herself to his side like kid glue. He'd spent most of the morning keeping her entertained by letting her climb up to her castle—in this case, huge round bales of hay—under his watchful eye. If he'd minded the make-believe, or the recollections the interaction had most surely produced, he hadn't let on. He'd just patiently played the knight to the imaginary queen, wielding an invisible sword while sporting a sadness in his eyes that couldn't be concealed, at least not from Hannah.

"How big is this place?" she asked when Marlene bent down and opened the door to the built-in beverage refrigerator.

"Eight bedrooms, at least ten baths, I think because I always lose count, and around 11,000 square feet."

She'd known the glorified log cabin was huge when they'd driven through the gates of the Big Blue, but not that huge. "You have enough room to establish your own commune."

Marlene smiled over one shoulder. "Would you like a glass of wine, dear?"

Hannah normally didn't drink in the middle of the day, but it was well after noon, so what the heck? "Sure, but just a little. I have to head home this evening."

"I'll pour just enough to take the edge off."

Hannah wanted to ask why on earth she should be edgy, yet when Marlene returned with the drinks, looking as solemn as a preacher, she assumed she would soon find out.

She accepted the wine and said, "Thanks," then took

a quick sip. The stuff was so dry it did little to wet her parched throat.

Marlene took a larger drink then held the glass's stem in a tight-fisted grasp, looking as if she could snap it in two. "You might be wondering why I asked you in here, Hannah."

That was a colossal understatement. "I assume it has something to do with Logan."

"Actually, no, it doesn't. It has to do with—"

"Mom, are you in there?"

Marlene sent her an apologetic look before responding to the summons. "Yes, Chance, I'm here."

The door opened wide to a six-foot-plus, brown-haired, athletically built man wearing a chambray shirt with the sleeves rolled up to his elbows, worn leather boots and faded jeans. "Just wondering if the coals are still hot on the grill."

"Yes, they are," Marlene said. "And Chance, this is Logan's new girl, Hannah. Hannah, this is my son, Chance, and if he doesn't learn to wipe his boots better at the back door, I'm going to ban him from the house."

Hannah wanted to correct her on the "Logan's girl" thing, but when Chance Lassiter turned his gaze on her, she was practically struck mute. She met eyes the exact same color of green as hers, and although his hair was a light shade of brown, the resemblance was uncanny. Not proof positive she could be a Lassiter, but pretty darn close.

She had enough wherewithal to set the glass down on the coffee table and offer her hand. "It's nice to meet you, Chance."

He leaned over and gave her hand a hearty shake.

"Pleasure's all mine," he said before regarding his mother again. "Did you have burgers or steak?"

Marlene shrugged. "Steaks, of course. What I always have when we have guests. I saved you one in the fridge to cook to your liking. Two flips on the grill and it's done." She turned her attention back to Hannah. "Chance owns and runs the whole ranching operation, including developing the cattle breeding program. He raises the best Black Angus in the country, but I hope you know that after sampling our steaks."

Fortunately she hadn't been formally introduced to the cows before she'd literally had them for lunch. "Unequivocally the best."

Chance grinned with pride. "We aim to please. So now I'm going to leave you ladies to your girl talk while I go grab a bite. I take it that little redheaded girl napping on the sofa beside Logan belongs to you, Hannah."

Clearly Cassie had finally wound down, a very good thing for the poor lawyer. "Yes, she's all mine, and she's quite a live wire."

"She's as pretty as her mama," he said. "Logan is one lucky guy. Think I'll go tell him that before I grab a bite and get back to riding the range."

Chance Lassiter could talk until he was blue in the face, but luck had nothing to do with their inevitable parting a few hours from now.

After Chance closed the door behind him, Hannah smiled at Marlene. "He seems to be a great guy. Is he your only child?"

"Yes, he is. And he's done very well considering he lost his father when he was only eight. I believe you were around six years old at the time."

How would she possibly know that? Unless… "Marlene, has Logan mentioned anything to you about why I'm here in Cheyenne?"

She momentarily looked away. "Yes, he has, but don't hold that against him because he was only trying to help."

Logan's determination to come to her aid only impressed Hannah more. "Then you know about the annuity J.D. bequeathed to me?"

"I do, although no one else in the family knows about it."

"And the nondisclosure I have to sign to accept it?"

"J.D. added that clause to protect me."

And that made no sense to Hannah. "Why would he feel the need to protect you?"

Marlene downed the rest of her wine and set the glass aside on the end table positioned between the chairs. "Because my husband, Charles, was your father."

Hannah's mind reeled from the shocking revelation, jarring loose a host of unanswered questions. "And you knew about this for how long?"

"Charles came to me and told me about his brief affair with Ruth a few days after he ended it," she said. "Both of us learned about the pregnancy two weeks after you were born."

She didn't know whether to apologize to Marlene for her mother's transgressions, or scold her for not saying something sooner. "And you're absolutely sure Charles was my father?"

"I demanded a paternity test, and when it confirmed he was without a doubt your dad, Charles insisted on being a part of your life."

Hannah took a moment to let that sink in. "Apparently that never happened since I don't remember any man claiming to be my father spending time with me."

Marlene fished a photo from the pocket of her slacks and handed it to her. "You were two years old when this was taken."

She could only stare at the lanky yet handsome cowboy seated on a park bench, a smiling little girl on his lap. She didn't recognize him, but she positively recognized herself. "I have no memories of this or him." And she hated that fact with a passion.

"That's because your mother quit allowing visits when Charles refused to leave me for her."

Her fury returned with the force of an exploding grenade. "She used me as a pawn?"

"Unfortunately, yes," Marlene said. "If Charles wouldn't give in to her demands, then she wouldn't let him see his daughter."

Hannah wasn't sure she could emotionally handle much more, but she had to ask. "And he didn't think to fight for me?"

"No, dear, that's not the case at all. Charles consulted several lawyers on several occasions through the years. Ironically, he even spoke with one family law attorney who used to work at Logan's firm. They all basically told him the same thing. A mother's rights, especially a mother who'd conceived a child and was essentially *dumped* by a married man, would trump the biological father's rights."

She couldn't fathom the time she'd lost getting to know her father, all because of the law. "That's archaic."

"That's the way it was in that day and time." Marlene laid a hand on Hannah's arm. "But Charles never stopped hoping that might change, and he never stopped sending you money up until his death. I took over the payments after that."

Hannah was rapidly approaching information overload. "My mother claimed my father never gave her a penny of support."

Marlene sent her a sympathetic look. "I am so sorry you're learning this now, but Ruth received a monthly check every month from the day you were born, until J.D. learned you'd left college and married, which she failed to tell him."

Obviously all-consuming bitterness had turned her mother into the consummate liar. "She failed to tell me any of this." And now for another pertinent question. "Do you happen to know why J.D. came to our house when I was in the first grade? I remembered him when Logan first approached me about the annuity and I did an internet search."

"He went to tell her about Charles's death in my stead," she said. "Ruth only wanted to know who was going to sign the check. J.D. insisted on contributing the full amount and then some, but I refused to let him. That's when he established the annuity in your name."

"But why on earth would he list my mother as the secondary beneficiary?"

"I assume he believed it would allow him control over the situation. I honestly believe he didn't want to create a scandal for me, since he didn't know Charles had confessed to me about the affair and you. Regardless of what my husband had done, Charles and J.D. were always thick as thieves."

And that left one very important consideration—

the wronged wife. "Marlene, I can't imagine what you went through all those years, knowing your husband created a baby with another woman. And then you were charitable enough to see to that child's welfare." Even if the child had never known. And how horrible to learn her own mother had betrayed her. At least now she knew how Ruth had come by the down payment for the house. A weak gesture in light of the lies.

"Believe me, Hannah," Marlene continued, "I'm no saint. It took me years to forgive Charles, and I resented the hell out of your mother. I also resented you in many ways, and for that I am greatly ashamed."

Hannah set the photo next to her wineglass and clasped Marlene's hand. "I don't blame you at all. I *do* blame my mother for the deceit. Although it does explain why she never seemed happy, especially not with me. No matter what I did, I never felt it was good enough."

"Yet somehow you turned out so well, dear," she said. "I can tell you're a wonderful mother and a genuinely good person. Believe me, Logan knows that, too."

Regardless, that wasn't going to be enough to keep him in her life. "Logan is a very good man with a wounded soul. I hope someday he realizes he deserves to be happy again."

"With your help, I'm sure he will."

If only that were true. "I hate to burst your bubble, Marlene, but when I leave here, I doubt I'll be coming back anytime soon."

Marlene frowned. "I was hoping you'd return now and then to get to know your brother."

Her brother. She'd been so embroiled in the details she hadn't given Chance a second thought. "Does he know about me?"

"No, but I plan to tell him in the very near future. And I hope you'll tell Logan how you really feel about him before you go."

Time to admit the agonizing truth. "He's only going to be a special man I had the pleasure of meeting, and that's all he'll ever be."

Marlene had the skeptical look down to a science. "Don't try to fool an old fool, Hannah. I can spot a woman in love at fifty paces."

Hannah fixed her gaze on the almost-full glass next to the photo, but she had no desire to drink, only sob. "It doesn't matter how I feel about him. Logan has all but given up on love. And that's sad when he needs it so very much."

"I'm asking you not to give up on him," Marlene said. "Men have been known to come around, once the woman of their dreams has flown the love nest. But before you do that, you need to tell him how the cow ate the cabbage and convince him that you're worth fighting for. Then make sure you turn around and leave so he'll have time to chew on it awhile."

"I suppose I could give that a shot."

"You'd be surprised how effective it can be."

Hannah could only hope. That's about all she had left to hold on to. Actually, that wasn't exactly the case. She picked up the photo and studied it again. "Do you mind if I keep this?"

"Not at all, dear." Marlene stood and smiled. "Now let's go find that hardheaded attorney so you can have the last word."

Hannah had the strongest feeling it could very well be her last stand.

* * *

"Looks like it's going to rain."

In response to Logan's observation, Hannah looked up. The overcast skies reflected her gloomy mood, but she needed to snap out of the funk in order to tell Logan exactly what had been brewing in her mind, with a little help from Marlene.

She kicked at a random stone as the two of them walked a path leading away from the house. "Hopefully it won't be more than a spring shower. Just enough rain that lasts long enough for Cassie to get in a good nap."

"Chance is hoping for a deluge."

"You mean my *half brother,* Chance?" she asked, as she took a glimpse to her right to gauge Logan's reaction.

"I figured Marlene told you everything."

His poker face and even tone told Hannah he'd been privy to that knowledge. "How long have you known Charles Lassiter was my father?"

"Since Wednesday."

"And you went three days without telling me?" She'd thought she'd meant more to him than that. Obviously she'd been wrong.

"Now before you get all worked up," he said, "Marlene made me promise I wouldn't say anything to you before she could explain. It was damn hard keeping you in the dark, but I had to respect her wishes."

She shrugged. "What's three days when compared to thirty years? I still cannot believe my own mother never told me about him, or the fact that she received checks from Charles and then Marlene during my formative years and beyond."

Finally, Logan showed something more than detachment to her disclosures. "That part I didn't know, Hannah. I'm sorry you had to find out after the fact."

She was sorry she couldn't change his mind about settling down. Or having children. Yet expecting someone to alter their ideals made little sense. "It's done, and I'm over it. I have a great daughter, own my home and a degree. Now I just need to find a job and my life will be complete." That rang false, even to Hannah's ears.

"You know, you could look for a job here," Logan said.

The suggestion took her aback, and gave her hope. "Why would I do that when my life is in Boulder?"

"So you can get to know your new family since you're not going to take the inheritance."

So much for hoping he might actually see a future with her. "That really only includes Chance, since I have no idea how my cousins will take the news." And who was to say her brother would even want to have a relationship with her?

"I still think that if you moved closer, we could get together every now and then."

Not at all what she wanted to hear. "For the occasional booty call?"

He scowled. "You know me well enough to know I respect you more than that. I just thought we could see where it goes."

She knew exactly where it would go. Nowhere. "Let's review, shall we? I eventually want to marry again and have at least one more child. You, on the other hand, would prefer to live your life alone, moving from one casual conquest to another with no commitment, in typical confirmed-bachelor fashion. And since I don't intend to follow in my mother's footsteps and wind up as someone's mistress, that puts us directly at odds. Do you not agree?"

He stopped in his tracks to stare at her, anger glinting in his dark eyes. "I've never seen you as some kind of conquest and definitely not as a potential mistress. I only thought that if we spent more time together—"

"You'd suddenly decide by some miracle to become a family man again?"

"I told you why—"

"You don't want to settle down. I know. You're too wrapped in guilt and grief to give me what I need. But what about *your* needs?"

He shifted his weight from one leg to the other. "What do you think I need?"

He'd asked for it, and she was glad to give it to him. "You need to get over yourself. You're not the only one who's lost someone they loved more than life itself. But life does go on unless you say it doesn't. And that's what you've been saying for the past eight years. Do you think keeping yourself closed off to all possibilities is honoring your daughter's memory? Believe me, it's doing just the opposite."

His eyes now reflected pent-up fury. "Leave Grace out of this."

"I can't, Logan, because deep down you know I'm right. And if I never see you again, it's going to be tough, and it's going to break my heart just like that memorial tattoo on your arm. But I'm not a quitter, and I didn't peg you as one, either, when I stupidly fell in love with you."

He looked astonished over her spontaneous admission. "You what?"

No need to stop when she was on a roll. "I love you.

Oh, I fought it with everything in me. I chalked it up to lust and liking your home theater. And of course my appreciation of your plumbing skills. What woman wouldn't want a man who could fix her leaky pipes? And I really valued your determination to make sure I found out the truth about my heritage." She hitched in a breath. "But do you know when I quit questioning my feelings?"

"No."

"Today, when I watched you playing with my daughter, and I saw this longing in your eyes that took my breath away. Whether you believe it or not, you're meant to be a father, and somewhere beneath that damned armor you've build around your heart, you want to be one again. But that will never happen unless you stop beating yourself up and being afraid of making a mistake."

Tension and silence hung between them despite the whistling wind. Hannah allowed the quiet for a few moments before she finished her diatribe. "Logan, I only want what's best for you, believe it or not. And I hate it that I hurt you by laying out the truth. I also pray you find the strength to love again. Maybe I'm not the woman you need, but you do need someone."

For the first time ever, he appeared to be rendered speechless. Either that, or he was simply too irate to speak.

When he failed to respond, Hannah decided to give up, though that went against her nature. But she wasn't too stubborn to recognize when it was time to throw in that towel. "If it's not too much of a bother, I'd like to go back to your place, collect my things and my car, and get back to Boulder before dark."

This time she didn't bother to wait for his answer. She simply spun around and headed back to the house to gather her child in order to go home and lick her wounds.

Yet as she afforded a glance over her shoulder, and she saw him standing there in the rain, looking forlorn instead of furious, she wondered if maybe she'd expected too much from Logan too soon. Given up on him too quickly. She wanted desperately to believe he might eventually come around to her side.

And that possibly could be too much to ask.

Yesterday afternoon, Logan had told Hannah goodbye after giving her and Cassie a brief hug, not once giving away the sorry state of his heart. Since then, he'd been carrying around a brand-new bushel full of regrets that kept running over and over in his head. He wound up spending the night seated on the floor in the now-vacant child's room, alone and lonely. He dozed off now and then, always awakening with a strong sense that he'd made the biggest mistake of his life when he let Hannah go without putting up a fight.

He'd blamed her for treading on his pride, when all she'd done was shine a light on the hard truth. In many ways, he had stopped living. But he hadn't stopped loving, because he was—without a doubt—in love with her. He loved her wit and her gentle ways. He loved the way she made love to him. He loved the fact she could melt his heart with only a smile. He hated that he hadn't uttered one word of that to her before she'd driven away, and now it might be too late.

Although he was dog-tired, that didn't keep him from sprinting down the stairs when he heard the doorbell chime. He hoped to see Hannah on his doorstep, but instead he peered through the peephole and found Chance Lassiter. As much as he liked and respected the guy, he wasn't in the mood for company. But when he noticed the wind had begun to push the rain beneath the portico, he decided he should probably let him in.

Logan opened the door and before he could mutter a greeting, Chance said, "You look like hell, Whittaker."

He ran a hand over his unshaven jaw and figured he looked like he'd wrestled a bear and lost. "Good to see you, too, Lassiter."

Chance stepped inside without an invite, shrugged off the heavy weatherproof jacket and shook it out, sprinkling drops of water all over the travertine tile. He then dug a pair of tiny blue socks from his jeans pocket and offered them to Logan. "Mom told me Cassie left these at the house. Is Hannah still here?"

He wished that were the case. "She went home yesterday afternoon."

"Damn. I really wanted to talk to her. When's she going to be back?"

"I don't think she'll be coming back anytime soon." Voicing it made the concept all too real. "At least not to see me."

"Trouble in paradise?"

Paradise had disappeared the minute she'd walked out his door. "Guess some things aren't meant to be."

"That's really too bad," Chance said. "I was hoping maybe you'd be my brother-in-law in the near future, that way I wouldn't hesitate to call you when I need help with the cows."

Chance's attempt at humor sounded forced to Logan, and with good reason. Suddenly learning you have a sister because your late father was a philanderer would be a damn bitter pill to swallow. "You don't hesitate to call me for help now, and I take it Marlene told you the whole story about your father and Hannah's mother."

"Yeah, the whole sorry story." Chance let go a caustic laugh. "You spend your life idolizing your dad, only to learn the guy was a good-for-nothing cheater. But at least I got a sibling out of the deal. That's if she wants to acknowledge me as her brother. Had I known the facts before she took off, I would've spoken with her yesterday while she was still at the ranch."

Had Logan known how bad he would hurt, he might not have let her take off. "I've got her phone number and address if you want to get in touch with her."

"I'll do that," he said. "Question is, what are you going to do about her?"

"I'm not sure what you mean."

Chance shook his head. "For a man with a whole lot of smarts, you're not real good at pretending to be stupid."

He didn't much care for the stupid designation, even if it might ring true in this instance. "Didn't know you planned to deliver insults along with the socks."

"Well, if the shoe fits, as Mom would say."

Logan also didn't appreciate the pun. "Look, Hannah and I had a good thing going, but now it's over."

Chance narrowed his eyes, looking like he was prepared to take his best shot, or throw a punch. "You do realize you're talking about my sister. If you used her and then threw her away like garbage, that's grounds to kick your ass."

"I don't use women and I sure as hell didn't use

Hannah, so simmer down. In fact, I stayed awake all night thinking about her."

Chance seemed satisfied by that response, at least satisfied enough to unclench his fists. He also looked a little too smug. "Man, do you have it bad for her."

Dammit, he'd walked right into that trap. "That's one hell of a major assumption, Lassiter."

"Are you going to tell me I'm wrong?"

Not unless he wanted to hand Chance one supersized lie. "No, you're not wrong."

"Well, hell, that sure explains why you look like something the mountain lion dragged in that the bloodhound couldn't stomach."

He really should have checked a mirror on his way downstairs. "Are you done deriding me now?"

"Nope. Not until you admit how you really feel about Hannah."

"I love her, dammit." There, he'd said it, and a hole in the tiled entry hadn't opened up and swallowed him. "Are you happy now?"

"As happy as a squirrel in the summer with a surplus of nuts. Do you still want to be with her?"

More than he could express. "Yeah, I do."

"Now what are you going to do about it?"

Logan didn't have a clue. "I'm sure you're itching to tell me."

"I don't even begin to understand what makes a woman tick," Chance began, "but I do know if you want her back, you've got to do it soon, before she has time to think about how you've wronged her."

"I'll call her as soon as I call my mom." Talk about serious avoidance.

Chance glared at him like he'd just proposed a plot

to commit murder. "Man, you can't do this over the phone. You have to go see her. Today."

"But—"

He pointed a finger in Logan's face. "You're going to show up at her house with something that will force her to forgive you."

"Flowers?"

"Yeah. Flowers are good, especially since it's Mother's Day. Do you have any planted in some garden?"

"Hell no. I'll have to buy them somewhere." Fortunately he had a connection who could accommodate him.

"What about one of those fancy silk suits?"

Logan's patience was wearing thin. "I'm an attorney, Chance. I have a damn suit."

"Sorry, but I had to ask because I've never seen you wear an entire suit, bud. Anyway, you'll show up in your suit with flowers—"

"For a die-hard bachelor, you're sure quick to dole out the advice."

"I just want my sister to be happy," Chance said in a surprisingly serious tone.

So did Logan. But would all the frills be enough to persuade Hannah to give them another chance? "What if she throws me out before I have my say?"

Chance slapped his back with the force of a steamroller. "Whittaker, according to Mom, Hannah loves you something awful, too. If you play your cards right, she'll let you come crawling back to her. Now I'm not saying you need to propose marriage because you've known each other a short time. My mom and dad only knew each other a month before they tied the knot and we now know how that one worked out."

Funny, Marlene hadn't mentioned that to Logan during their many conversations. "No kidding? Only a month?"

"No kidding," he said. "And then he cheated on his wife, not that I think you'd do that to Hannah."

"Not on your life." She was all he needed. All he would ever need.

"And to top it off," Chance continued, "Mom told me yesterday that in spite of my father's faults and weakness, she never doubted his love for her. It's just hard for me to believe love that strong exists."

Logan was beginning to believe it existed between him and Hannah, provided she hadn't fallen out of love with him overnight. "I hope you eventually forgive Marlene. She was just trying to protect you from the ugly truth."

"I'll forgive her eventually," Chance said. "As far as my dad's concerned, I'm not sure that will ever happen."

Logan knew all about that inability to forgive, and he could only hope Chance eventually came around like he had. But Hannah… "I hope like hell Hannah forgives me for taking so long to realize we need to be together."

"She'll forgive you the minute you show up at her door wearing your heart on your sleeve."

"Guess that's better than eating crow."

"You'll be doing that, too, Whittaker, so pack some salt. And groveling couldn't hurt. Hope that suit isn't too expensive in case you have to get down on your knees when you beg."

The suit didn't mean as much to him as Hannah. His pride no longer mattered much where she was concerned, either. "Are you sure you don't want to go with me, Lassiter? In case you want to talk with her after I do."

Chance grinned, grabbed his coat and backed toward the door. "You're on your own with this one, bud. Now go get a shower and shave, then go get your girl. Who knows? She might even be waiting for you."

Ten

Hannah walked out the door to meet Gina for their traditional Mother's Day brunch, only to stop short of the sidewalk when she caught sight of the black Mercedes parked at the curb. And leaning against that sedan's driver's door was the beautiful, wounded, brown-eyed man who'd invaded her thoughts the majority of the night. He wore a beige silk suit with matching tie and a white tailored shirt, a bouquet of roses in one hand, a piece of white paper in the other. If not for the dress cowboy boots, she might believe this was Logan Whittaker's clone. Yet when he grinned, showing those dimples to supreme advantage, that was all the confirmation she needed. But why was he here? She aimed to find out.

Hannah stepped across the yard, her three-inch heels digging into the grass made moist by the deluge that had arrived during the night. Fortunately the clouds had begun to break up, allowing the sun to peek through.

When she reached Logan, she shored up her courage and attempted a smile. "What are you doing here, Mr. Whittaker?"

"Thought you might need a plumber."

"My pipes appear to be holding, so no more water in the floor." On the other hand, her heart was flooded with a love for him that just wouldn't leave her be. "Since you're wearing a suit, I thought maybe you got lost on your way to some wedding."

"Nope, but I was pretty lost until I found you."

Her flooded heart did a little flip-flop in her chest. But she wasn't ready to give in to his pretty words and patent charms. Yet. "Who are the flowers for?"

"You," he said as he handed them off to her. "Happy Mother's Day."

She brought the roses to her nose and drew in the scent. "Thank you."

He leaned around her. "Where's Cassie?"

"Two houses down at the Romeros'. She's going to spend a few hours there while Gina and I have lunch together."

"Who's going to be watching her?"

His protective tone both surprised and pleased Hannah. "Gina's husband, Frank. He's used to watching their baby and the girls when Gina and I have plans."

"That sounds like a damn daunting job."

"He's a great dad, but he's had lots of practice." *And you would be a great dad, too,* she wanted to say.

Amazingly the familiar sadness didn't show in his eyes. "I guess practice makes perfect."

He still had a lot to learn. "Not perfect, Logan. No parent is ever perfect."

"I'm starting to realize that."

Oh, how she wanted to believe him. Yet she continued to resist the notion he had finally seen the light.

Hannah pointed at the document now clenched in his fist. "What's that?"

"The annuity terms that include the nondisclosure clause." He unfolded the paper, tore it in half and then tossed the remains into the open back window. "And according to your wishes, it's no longer valid."

Hannah couldn't resist teasing him a little. "Darn. I decided last night to sign it and take the money."

"Are you serious?"

She stifled a laugh. "No, I'm not serious. I could always use that kind of money, but I have everything I need without it, especially since Cassie's future is secure, thanks to my in-laws."

He inclined his head and looked at her as if he could see right through her phony assertion. "Everything?"

Except for those things money couldn't buy—like his love. "Enough to get by until I find a job. And mark my words, I will find a job even if I have to flip burgers."

"Marlene told me there's an opening at one of the rural high schools between my place and the Big Blue. They need a biology teacher. You should go for it."

"You're saying I should just uproot my child, sell my house and move to the middle of nowhere?"

"As I mentioned earlier, you'd have the opportunity to get to know your brother. We can continue to get to know each other better, too."

And he would have to do better than that. "We've already had this discussion, Logan. I want—"

"A man who can promise you a solid future and more kids."

"Exactly."

Some unnamed emotion reflected in his eyes. "I can be that man, Hannah. God knows I want to be."

The declaration tossed her into an emotional tailspin. "If that's true, then what made you suddenly change your mind?"

"What you told me about not honoring Grace's memory. I sat up all night in that room with the princesses on the wall and had a long talk with my daughter, as crazy as it seems."

How many times had she had those conversations with Danny in the distant past? "It's not crazy at all. It's long overdue."

"Anyway, for the first time since the funeral, I cried like a baby. But that meltdown didn't occur last night only because of Gracie. It had a lot to do with losing you."

Hannah could tell the admission was costing him as much as it was costing her. She wanted to throw her arms around him, tell him it would be okay, but she wasn't quite ready to do that yet. "Are you sure you're prepared to make a commitment to me and Cassie if and when the time comes?"

"I'm all in, Hannah," he said adamantly. "I also know I can be a good dad to Cassie. And do you want to know how I figured that one out?"

"Yes, I would."

He looked down and toed a random clump of grass before bringing his gaze back to hers. "When I was playing with Cassie yesterday on the hay bales, she slipped a few times and I caught her. Once I couldn't reach her, but she managed to pick herself back up after she tumbled to the bottom. Granted, it scared the hell out of me for a few minutes, but it also made me acknowledge that kids are actually pretty resilient, and the truth is, you can't logically be there for your children all the time." He exhaled roughly. "You can only do the best you can to protect them, and sadly sometimes that isn't enough, but you can't spend your life being paralyzed by a fear of failure."

A lesson everyone should learn. Unfortunately, he'd learned it the hard way. "Cassie's completely enamored of you, Logan. She told me on the drive home that you would make a good daddy, and she's right. But I've known that all along. I'm just glad you finally realized it."

His smile was soft and sincere. "She still thinks I'm some kind of prince."

"So do I. Or maybe I should say a prince in progress. You still need some work, but the flowers helped your cause."

He reached over and clasped her hand. "If I tell you I can't imagine my life without you, would that help, too?"

Hannah held back the tears, with great effort. "Immensely."

He brought her closer. "How about if I tell you I love you?"

So much for keeping those tears at bay. "Really?"

He gently kissed her cheek. "Really. I didn't expect to fall so hard and so fast for someone, because I never have. Hell, I didn't expect you at all. And although neither of us knows what the future will bring, I do know what I want."

Hannah sniffed and hoped she didn't look like a raccoon. "For me to buy waterproof mascara from now on?"

He responded with that smile she had so grown to

adore. "No. I want to give us a fighting chance. I promise to do everything in my power to make it work."

"I promise that, too." And she did, with all her heart and soul. "I love you, Logan."

"I love you, too, sweetheart."

Then he kissed her, softly, slowly, sealing the vow they'd made at that moment, and those vows Hannah believed were yet to come.

"I guess this means brunch is off."

She broke the kiss to find Gina standing in the middle of the sidewalk, gawking. "I suppose we'll have to postpone until next year."

Gina shrugged. "That's probably for the best. Frank's been complaining of a cold all morning and Trey's teething. I'd feel guilty if I left him with three kids, and even more guilty if I spoiled this wonderful little reunion. However, it does pain me to break a long-standing tradition."

"Tell you what, Gina," Logan said as he kept his arms around Hannah. "If you'll let me take my lady to lunch, I'll give you and your husband a night on the town, my treat. We'll even keep the kids."

Gina's eyes went as wide as saucers. "How about tonight? That would so cure Frank of what ails him."

He returned his attention back to Hannah. "Works for me, if it works for you."

With one exception. "Sure, as long as we have a few hours alone before we're left in charge of the troops."

"It's a deal," Gina said as she backed up a few steps. "Have a good lunch, and have some of that wild monkey sex for dessert, too."

As soon as her friend left the immediate premises, Hannah gave Logan another quick kiss. "You're mighty brave, taking on three kids."

He responded with a grin. "Hey, I've got to get into practice for when we have our three. Or maybe four."

Sweet, welcome music to Hannah's ears. "Don't get ahead of yourself, buster. You'll have to marry me first, Logan Whittaker, my repressed plumber."

"You know, Hannah Armstrong, my maid-in-waiting, I just might do that sooner than you think."

The past six weeks had whirled by in a flurry of changes. She'd sold the house, moved into the Big Blue for the sake of her minor child, spent every day with Logan, and even a few nights alone with him, thanks to Marlene's generosity. Aside from that, the saintly woman hadn't even flinched when Cassie had begun to call her Grandma.

Best of all, Hannah had learned that morning she'd been awarded the high school biology teaching job and would begin in the fall. Things couldn't be going any better, and tonight she and Logan planned to celebrate with a night on the town and a hotel stay in Denver. But she'd better hurry up with the preparations, otherwise Logan might leave without her.

On that thought, she inserted the diamond earrings he'd given her two weeks ago on the one-month anniversary of their meeting. Admittedly, and ridiculously, she'd secretly hoped for jewelry that fit on her left ring finger, but she had no doubt that would eventually come. She had no doubts whatsoever about their future.

After a quick dab of lipstick and a mirror check to make sure the white satin dress was properly fitted, Hannah grabbed her clutch in one hand and slipped the overnight bag's strap over one bare shoulder. She then rushed out of the bedroom and down the hall of the wing she shared with Marlene.

She was somewhat winded when she reached the staircase, and her breath deserted her completely when she saw Logan standing at the bottom landing. He'd donned a black tuxedo with a silver tie, and he was actually wearing Italian loafers, not the usual Western boots.

She couldn't help but smile as she floated down the stairs and took his extended hand when she reached the bottom. "Okay, what did you do with my cowboy lawyer?"

"According to your daughter, tonight I'm supposed to be a prince. This is as close as I could get because I refuse to wear those damn tights and a codpiece."

She reached up and kissed his neck. "I'd buy tickets to see you in tights."

He sent her a champion scowl. "Save your money 'cause it ain't happenin'."

"That's too bad."

He grinned. "You like bad, especially when it comes to me."

Oh, yeah. "I won't argue with that."

He crooked his arm for her to take. "Are you ready, Ms. Armstrong?"

"I am, Prince Logan. Take me away."

Instead of heading toward the front door, Logan guided Hannah down the corridor and into the great room, where an unexpected crowd had gathered. A crowd consisting of Marlene wearing a beautiful white chiffon dress, Chance dressed in a navy shirt and dark jeans, Cassie decked out in her pink princess gown, complete with pretty coat and feather boa, and of all people, senior law partner, Walter Drake, who had debonair down pat. Hannah had to wonder if they were going to pile all these people into a car caravan and head to Denver together.

"Did you plan a party without me knowing?" she asked when Logan positioned her next to the floor-to-ceiling stone fireplace.

"That's somewhat accurate," Logan said. "And you're the guest of honor."

A frenzy of applause rang out, accompanied by a few ear-piercing whistles, compliments of Chance. Her half brother had become very special to her, and he'd proven to be a stellar uncle to Cassie, evidenced by the fact he'd picked up his niece and held her in his arms.

"First, thank you all for being here," Logan began, sounding every bit the attorney, with a little Texas accent thrown in. "But before we get to the celebration, I have something important to ask a very special lady."

Surely he wasn't going to… Hannah held her breath so long she thought her chest might explode, until Logan said, "Cassie, come here."

While Logan took a seat on the raised heart, Chance lowered Cassie to the ground. She ran over as fast as her little pink patent leather shoes allowed. She then came to a sliding stop, plopped herself down in Logan's lap and draped her tiny arms around his neck.

"Darlin'," Logan began, "you know I love your mama, and I love you, right?"

She nodded emphatically, causing her red ringlets to bounce. "Uh-huh."

"And you know that I'm never going to try to take your daddy's place."

"My Heaven daddy."

"That's right. But I sure would like to be your daddy here on earth, if that's okay."

"I'd like you to be my earth daddy, too," Cassie said.

Hannah placed a hand over her mouth to stifle a sob when she saw the look of sheer love in both Cassie's and Logan's eyes.

Logan kissed her daughter's forehead before setting her back on her feet. "Now I have to ask your mom a few questions."

Cassie responded with a grin. "You betcha." She then looked up at Hannah, who could barely see due to the moisture clouding her eyes. "I told you so, Mama. Logan is your prince."

Cassie ran back to her uncle while Logan came to his feet. He moved right in front of Hannah, his gaze unwavering. "Sweetheart, I want to wake up with you every morning and go to bed with you every night. I want to find a good balance between work and family. I don't want to replace Cassie's real dad, but I want to be the best father I can be to her. And I want, God willing, for your face to be the last one I see before I'm gone from this earth. Therefore, if you'll have me, Hannah Armstrong, I want more than anything for you to be my wife."

The room had grown so silent, Hannah would swear everyone could hear her pounding heart. This was no time for smart remarks. For questions or doubts. This precious request Logan had made only required one answer. "Yes, I will be your wife."

Following a kiss, and more applause, Logan pulled a black velvet box from his inner pocket and opened it to a brilliant, emerald-cut diamond ring flanked by more diamonds. "This should seal the deal," he said as he removed it from the holder, pocketed the box again, then placed it on her left finger.

Hannah held it up to the light. "Heavens, Logan Whittaker, this could rival the Rocky Mountains. I might have to wear a sling to hold it up."

Logan leaned over and whispered, "Always the smart-ass, and I love it. I love you."

She sent him a wily grin. "I love you, too, and I really and truly love the ring."

The pop of the cork signaled the party had begun as Marlene started doling out champagne to everyone of legal age. When Cassie asked, "Can I have some?" Logan and Hannah barked out, "No!" simultaneously.

She turned to Logan and smiled. "You're going to come in handy when she turns sixteen and the boys come calling."

"She's not going to date until she's twenty-one," he said in a gruff tone.

"And I'm the Princess of Romania," she replied, although tonight she did feel like a princess. A happy, beloved princess, thanks to her unpredictable prince.

Following a few toasts, many congratulations and a lot of hugs and kisses, Logan finally escorted Hannah out the door and into the awaiting black limousine, just one more surprise in her husband-to-be's repertoire. Then again, everything about her relationship with Logan had been one gigantic surprise.

After they were seated side by side, and the partition dividing the front and back of the car had been raised, Logan kissed her with all the passion they'd come to know in each other's arms.

"How did you enjoy that proposal?" he asked once they'd come up for air.

"It was okay. I really hoped you would have dressed like a plumber and presented the ring on a wrench."

He grinned. "Would you have worn a maid's uniform?"

"Sure. And I'd even pack a feather duster."

The levity seemed to subside when Logan's expression turned serious. "I've set up a trust fund in Cassie's name, in case you want to tell your former in-laws thanks, but no thanks."

"I'd be glad to tell them to take their trust fund and control and go to Hades. And if I did, frankly I don't think they'd care. But if they do decide they want to see her again, it wouldn't be fair to keep her from them." The same way she'd been kept from her father.

"We'll deal with it when and if the time comes. Together." Logan pulled an open bottle of champagne from the onboard ice bucket, then filled the two available glasses. "To our future and our family."

Hannah tipped her crystal flute against his. "And to weddings. Which reminds me, when are we going to do it?"

He laid his free hand on her thigh. "The seat back here is pretty big, so I say let's do it now."

Spoken like a man who'd spent a lot of time with a wise-cracker. She gave him an elbow in the side for good measure. "I meant, as if you didn't know, when are we going to get married?"

He faked a disappointed look that melted into an endearing smile. "I'm thinking maybe on July Fourth."

That allowed Hannah very little time to plan. But since this would be both their second marriages, it wouldn't require anything elaborate. "You know something? People will speculate I'm pregnant if we have the ceremony that soon."

He nuzzled her neck and blew softly in her ear. "Let's just give them all something to talk about."

Lovely. More rumors, as if the Lassiter family hadn't had enough of that lately. Oh, well. It certainly kept things interesting. So did Logan's talented mouth. "Then July Fourth it is. We can even have fireworks."

He winked. "Fireworks on Independence Day for my beautiful independent woman works well for me."

An independent woman and single mom, and a onetime secret heiress, who'd had the good fortune to fall in love with a man who had given her an incredible sense of freedom.

Now, as Hannah gazed at her gorgeous new fiancé, this onetime secret heiress was more than ready for the lifetime celebration to begin. Starting now.

* * * * *

DYNASTIES: THE LASSITERS
Don't miss a single story!

THE BLACK SHEEP'S INHERITANCE
by Maureen Child
FROM SINGLE MOM TO SECRET HEIRESS
by Kristi Gold
EXPECTING THE CEO'S CHILD
by Yvonne Lindsay
LURED BY THE RICH RANCHER
by Kathie DeNosky
TAMING THE TAKEOVER TYCOON
by Robyn Grady
REUNITED WITH THE LASSITER BRIDE
by Barbara Dunlop

COMING NEXT MONTH FROM

HARLEQUIN®

Desire

Available June 3, 2014

#2305 MY FAIR BILLIONAIRE
by Elizabeth Bevarly

To land his biggest deal, self-made billionaire Peyton needs to convince high society he's one of them. With help from Ava, his old nemesis, Peyton transforms himself, but is it him or his makeover that captures Ava's heart?

#2306 EXPECTING THE CEO'S CHILD
Dynasties: The Lassiters • by Yvonne Lindsay

When celeb CEO Dylan Lassiter learns Jenny's pregnant after their one night together, he proposes. To keep her past a secret, media-shy Jenny refuses him. But Dylan will only accept "I do" for an answer!

#2307 BABY FOR KEEPS
Billionaires and Babies • by Janice Maynard

Wealthy Dylan Kavanagh loves being a hero, so when single mom Mia needs help, Dylan offers her a room—at his place. But close proximity soon has Dylan thinking about making this little family his—for keeps.

#2308 THE TEXAN'S FORBIDDEN FIANCÉE
Lone Star Legends • by Sara Orwig

Jake and Madison once loved each other, until their families' feud tore them apart. Now, years later, the sexy rancher is back, wanting Madison's oil-rich ranch—and the possibility of a second chance!

#2309 A BRIDE FOR THE BLACK SHEEP BROTHER
At Cain's Command • by Emily McKay

To succeed in business, Cooper Larson strikes a deal with his former sister-in-law, the perfect society woman. When sparks fly, they're both shocked, but Cooper will have to risk everything to prove it's her and not her status he covets.

#2310 A SINFUL SEDUCTION
by Elizabeth Lane

When wealthy philanthropist Cal Jeffords tracks down the woman he believes embezzled millions from his foundation, he only wants the missing money. Then he wants her. But can he trust her innocence?

YOU CAN FIND MORE INFORMATION ON UPCOMING HARLEQUIN® TITLES, FREE EXCERPTS AND MORE AT WWW.HARLEQUIN.COM.

HDCNM0514

REQUEST YOUR FREE BOOKS!
2 FREE NOVELS PLUS 2 FREE GIFTS!

HARLEQUIN® *Desire*

ALWAYS POWERFUL, PASSIONATE AND PROVOCATIVE

YES! Please send me 2 FREE Harlequin Desire® novels and my 2 FREE gifts (gifts are worth about $10). After receiving them, if I don't wish to receive any more books, I can return the shipping statement marked "cancel." If I don't cancel, I will receive 6 brand-new novels every month and be billed just $4.55 per book in the U.S. or $4.99 per book in Canada. That's a savings of at least 13% off the cover price! It's quite a bargain! Shipping and handling is just 50¢ per book in the U.S. and 75¢ per book in Canada.* I understand that accepting the 2 free books and gifts places me under no obligation to buy anything. I can always return a shipment and cancel at any time. Even if I never buy another book, the two free books and gifts are mine to keep forever.

225/326 HDN F4ZC

Name	(PLEASE PRINT)	
Address		Apt. #
City	State/Prov.	Zip/Postal Code

Signature (if under 18, a parent or guardian must sign)

Mail to the **Harlequin® Reader Service**:
IN U.S.A.: P.O. Box 1867, Buffalo, NY 14240-1867
IN CANADA: P.O. Box 609, Fort Erie, Ontario L2A 5X3

Want to try two free books from another line?
Call 1-800-873-8635 or visit www.ReaderService.com.

* Terms and prices subject to change without notice. Prices do not include applicable taxes. Sales tax applicable in N.Y. Canadian residents will be charged applicable taxes. Offer not valid in Quebec. This offer is limited to one order per household. Not valid for current subscribers to Harlequin Desire books. All orders subject to credit approval. Credit or debit balances in a customer's account(s) may be offset by any other outstanding balance owed by or to the customer. Please allow 4 to 6 weeks for delivery. Offer available while quantities last.

Your Privacy—The Harlequin® Reader Service is committed to protecting your privacy. Our Privacy Policy is available online at www.ReaderService.com or upon request from the Harlequin Reader Service.

We make a portion of our mailing list available to reputable third parties that offer products we believe may interest you. If you prefer that we not exchange your name with third parties, or if you wish to clarify or modify your communication preferences, please visit us at www.ReaderService.com/consumerschoice or write to us at Harlequin Reader Service Preference Service, P.O. Box 9062, Buffalo, NY 14269. Include your complete name and address.

Read on for a sneak peek at USA TODAY *bestselling author
Yvonne Lindsay's EXPECTING THE CEO'S CHILD,
the third novel in Harlequin Desire's
DYNASTIES: THE LASSITERS series.*

*CEO restaurateur Dylan Lassiter is in for a big surprise from
a fling he can't forget…*

The sound of the door buzzer alerted Jenna to a customer out front. She pasted a smile on her face and walked out into the showroom only to feel the smile freeze in place as she recognized Dylan Lassiter, in all his decadent glory, standing with his back to her, his attention apparently captured by the ready-made bouquets she kept in the refrigerated unit along one wall.

Her reaction was instantaneous—heat, desire and shock each flooded her in turn. The last time she'd seen him had been in the coat closet where they'd impulsively sought refuge, releasing the sexual energy that had ignited so dangerously and suddenly between them.

"Can I help you?" she asked, feigning a lack of recognition right up until the moment he turned around and impaled her with those cerulean-blue eyes of his.

Her mouth dried. It was a crime against nature that any man could look so beautiful and so masculine all at the same time.

A hank of softly curling hair fell across his high forehead, making her hand itch to smooth it back, to then trace the stubbled line of his jaw.

She'd spent the past two and a half months in a state of disbelief at her actions. It had literally been a one-night *stand*, she reminded herself cynically. The coat closet hadn't allowed for anything else. Her body still remembered every second of how he'd made her feel—and reacted in kind again.

"Jenna," Dylan acknowledged with a slow nod of his head, his gaze not moving from her face for a second.

"Dylan," she said, feigning surprise. "What brings you back to Cheyenne?"

The instant she said the words she silently groaned. Of course he was here for the opening of his new restaurant. The local chamber of commerce—heck, the whole town—was abuzz with the news. She'd tried to ignore anything Lassiter-related for weeks now, but there was no ignoring the man in front of her.

The father of her unborn child.

Don't miss EXPECTING THE CEO'S CHILD
by Yvonne Lindsay, available June 2014.

Wherever Harlequin® Desire
books and ebooks are sold.

HARLEQUIN®

Desire

ALWAYS POWERFUL, PASSIONATE AND PROVOCATIVE.

BABY FOR KEEPS
Billionaires and Babies
by Janice Maynard

"I have a proposition for you."

Wealthy Dylan Kavanagh loves being a hero, so when single mom Mia needs help, Dylan offers her a room—at his place. But close proximity soon has Dylan thinking about making this little family his—for keeps.

Look for
BABY FOR KEEPS
in June 2014, from Harlequin® Desire!
Wherever books and ebooks are sold.

Don't miss other scandalous titles from the
Billionaires and Babies miniseries,
available now wherever books and ebooks are sold.

Billionaires and Babies: Powerful men…wrapped around their babies' little fingers

HARLEQUIN®

Desire

ALWAYS POWERFUL, PASSIONATE AND PROVOCATIVE.

MY FAIR BILLIONAIRE
by Elizabeth Bevarly

**She was still classy. She was still beautiful.
She was still out of his league.**

In high school, Ava may have been Payton's personal mean girl by day, but a different kind of spark flew at night. Now the tables have turned and Payton's about to make his first billion while Ava's living a bit more humbly. He needs her to teach him how to pass in high society, if they can manage to put old rivalries to bed. It's clear to both that chemistry wasn't just for second period, but will Payton still want her when he learns about the scandal that sent Ava from riches to rags?

Look for
MY FAIR BILLIONAIRE
by Elizabeth Bevarly, in June 2014 from,
Harlequin® Desire.

HARLEQUIN®

Desire

ALWAYS POWERFUL, PASSIONATE AND PROVOCATIVE.

A BRIDE FOR THE BLACK SHEEP BROTHER

At Cain's Command

by Emily McKay

"I don't think I'm the right woman for you."

To succeed in business, Cooper Larson strikes a deal with his former sister-in-law, the perfect society woman. Cooper's hunger for his former sister-in-law hasn't abated over the years. When sparks fly, they're both shocked, but Cooper will have to risk everything to prove it's her and not her status he covets.

Look for
A BRIDE FOR THE BLACK SHEEP BROTHER
in June 2014, from Harlequin® Desire!

Wherever books and ebooks are sold.

Don't miss other exciting titles from the
At Cain's Command miniseries by Emily McKay,
available now wherever ebooks are sold.

ALL HE REALLY NEEDS
ALL HE EVER WANTED

HD73322